PARENTING FROM THE HEART

A Guide to the Essence of Parenting

Jack Pransky, Ph.D.

© 1997, 1998, 2001

NorthEast Health Realization Institute
234 Pransky Rd.
Cabot, VT 05647
(802) 563-2730

Third Edition: January 2001
Third printing: April 1999
Second edition: May 1998
First edition: October 1997

Typesetting and Design by Russell Smith
Editing by Martha Gagliardi
Illustrations by Shirley H. Pransky
Cover drawing by Jaime E. Pransky

Library of Congress Cataloging-in-Publication Data
Pransky, Jack B.
        Parenting from the Heart / Jack Pransky – 3rd ed.
        p. cm.
ISBN 1-58820-383-2
1. Parents/parenting 2. Health Realization 3. Psychology of Mind 4.
Prevention 5. Resiliency
I. Title
Library of Congress Catalog Card Number: 97-92271
1997 CIP

This book is printed on acid free paper

Praise for Jack Pransky's *Prevention: The Critical Need:*

I commend [this book] to anyone who is genuinely concerned about
doing something effective about preventing social problems and mental
disorders in this country. This book will establish him among the stars
of public health and primary prevention.
George Albee, Ph.D.

1st Books – rev. 01/26/01

To the lights of my life: Judy, David, and Jaime.

Acknowledgments

Very special thanks to~

Dr. H. Stephen Glenn for helping me to be a far more effective parent.

Dr. George S. Pransky and Dr. Roger C. Mills for showing a new way.

Russell Smith for his book production work, and Martha Gagliardi for her editorial help.

Shirley Pransky, my mother, for providing the illustrations–and to both my mother and father for raising me so well.

And especially to Judy, David, and Jaime, for their contributions, and for everything!

Author's Note

This approach to parenting is based upon an understanding that is often called Health Realization, which is described throughout this book.

It was brought to light by philosopher Sydney Banks, then translated into a psychological approach by Dr. George Pransky and Dr. Roger Mills through their study of what makes mentally healthy people healthy. They learned how others can incorporate into their lives what mentally healthy people understand. When parents gain this understanding, they see their children and teenagers with new eyes and begin to act toward them in ways that draw out their mental health.

What I have learned from this understanding cannot be measured in words. I have incorporated it into my life. It has become part of who I am and what I know.

What I have learned about parenting from Drs. Pransky and Mills has become so enmeshed in me that it is now difficult to attribute the source of specific points. This has posed a dilemma in writing this book. Thus, except for specific quotes and where I am certain that the content did not arise from my own insights, I did not cite credit for specific items. Yet, Dr. Mills and Dr. Pransky deserve much of the credit! The same can be said for Dr. H. Steven Glenn in the Appendix.

FOREWORD

H. Stephen Glenn

For over thirty years I have studied issues involved in raising children and preparing them for the challenges of life. During this time I have conducted thousands of workshops seminars and courses for parents, foster parents, stepparents and educators. Through this experience, it has become increasingly apparent that the majority of people, faced with the challenges of child rearing, often look to "experts" for direction, techniques and often "the answers" to the endless questions that arise in working with children.

While it is always appropriate to seek *wisdom*, it is also true that every relationship is a unique synthesis of dynamic and constantly changing variables in which *inspiration* is often as important as knowledge. The challenge of balancing heart and head is like an endless walk down a tightrope in which knowledge helps us know what needs to be done and the heart provides the balance necessary to do it under the pressures of each moment. Learning to live in and trust our *inner light* is particularly difficult for those of us raised in the western world during the scientific era (which is only now giving way to the "relationship era").

In *Parenting From the Heart*, Jack Pransky offers practical wisdom grounded in intimate experiences with his own children. Most clearly, the message of being open and respectful comes through in the emphasis on collaborative problem solving and family management. The principles of creativity, commitment, and patience will enrich any relationship, but are of unusual significance in guiding children through a world of increasingly transient relationships and "quick-fixes," which are so characteristic of modern society.

In an era in which media often overwhelms us with the weird, the bazaar, the negative and often the frightening aspects of human health and behavior, it is refreshing to celebrate with Jack the innate goodness and potential for healthy living that lies within humanity. To see these qualities within children and nurture them in body, mind and spirit so that *health realization* can express itself as spontaneous element of life is one of the greatest contributions one generation can make to the next. Remember, "Hope dies in the face of pessimism...but springs eternally from the awareness and celebration of positive alternatives!"

While the rate and intensity with which knowledge, technology and lifestyle are changing has created a world without reliable maps or guideposts, the compass of a clear mind and an open heart provides unique direction and light within the chaos. The wise and practical steps offered in this book provide comfort and support for those of us who are open to raising children as a process in which our children are also teachers and fellow travelers.

Over the years I have become increasingly concerned over the number of books and courses on childrearing that are prescriptive in nature and that offer "the way" to deal with various issues that are inevitable in working with children. It has been my experience every child is a unique person and every relationship is unique and constantly changing. Therefore, an appropriate response to a given issue, with a given child, at a given moment may be totally inappropriate for that same child (let alone another) under different circumstances.

While most people seek the security of a cookbook, anyone who has tried to use one knows that sooner or later you end up changing a recipe to reflect your own needs and tastes. On this important issue, Jack Pransky takes the high road and offers support and guidelines for those with the courage to live and grow in the process of life-touching-life. He resists the temptation to rescue us by offering *his* solutions, and, instead, models the principles that the book advocates by encouraging us to discover *our own*. Perhaps it should be said that this book is "not for the faint of heart!"

TABLE OF CONTENTS

PREFACE

This is not the book it started to be.

For ten years I had run many parenting courses and trained many parenting course instructors. For my book, *Prevention: The Critical Need*, I had thoroughly researched every known theory on parenting that I could find. I believed I knew most everything one could know about the subject. In my own home I had successfully put into practice what I had learned. I intended to write a book titled, "The Pocket Encyclopedia of Parenting and Discipline" that would cut through to the essentials of all known parenting theories and techniques, list problem situations parents most often encounter with their children, and offer solutions based on those theories and techniques.

I then stumbled upon an approach that was so new and different and so much more effective that I had to question everything I thought I knew. This shocked me, for this new approach had emerged not from any parenting theory but from what could be called a "new" understanding of how the human mind functions to cause people (parents and children included) to feel and behave as they do.

Previously I had been saying, "Parenting is the toughest job any of us can do." Yet, this new approach made parenting seem, comparatively, so effortless and joyful. The way I had been trained, there always seemed to be so much to remember to do. Despite my knowledge and skill I found it difficult to always stay on top of the right technique to use in a given situation, especially when I was overwrought about something.

I am not at all suggesting that what I had learned previously was a bad idea or a waste of time; on the contrary, it helped me develop a good relationship with my own children. However, when I decided to test out this new approach on my family, low and behold, our relationships markedly improved–and it seemed so much easier! At first I thought this approach too simple. But it worked! The reason? It pointed me within. It told me to put aside all the techniques I had learned and, instead, tuned me into what my heart told me to do.

While one or two sets of tapes had been developed on this approach—and I highly recommend them [see Bibliography]—when I began writing this no book about applying this approach to parenting had yet been written.* I set aside my "Pocket Encyclopedia," for I knew in my heart that this new approach was right and would be far more valuable.

I have found this to be the happiest and most productive way to deal with children and teenagers. To date, unfortunately, it has been the best-kept secret in parenting. I hope it no longer will be. Enjoy!

Jack Pransky
Cabot, VT
September, 1997
(revised, June, 2000)

----

*Note: Since then, Mills (1995) published the *Health Realization Parent Manual.*

INTRODUCTION

No set of discipline techniques will give you a good relationship with your children.

Discipline techniques are only fine-tuning mechanisms. As on a television set the fine-tuning knob will only work when the signal is strong enough. The feeling is the signal.

The feeling is what we feel in our hearts, and the relationships we build. This book goes beyond techniques to the feeling. If the right feeling is not present, our discipline will not work. At best we will get temporary, begrudging compliance.

In essence, two understandings lie at the heart of parenting:

1. Our children always carry within them all the mental health and well-being, wisdom and common sense they will ever need. It only needs to be drawn out and nurtured in the kind of loving environment that will help it flourish.

2. Our children can access this innate health and wisdom by understanding that they have it, by seeing how they think in ways that keep them from realizing it, and by quieting or clearing their minds of such thinking so their health and wisdom are unveiled and available to guide their lives.

The same is true for parents. We can access our health, well-being, and wisdom at any time to guide our parenting.

As trees in a forest naturally gravitate toward the light, when we create the kind of environment that draws out this natural health and wisdom, we naturally guide our children in healthy ways and away from unproductive feelings and disruptive behaviors.

In a nutshell, that is what this book is about

I. LIVING IN AN ENVIRONMENT OF LOVE AND POSITIVE FEELINGS

"You don't understand kids!" my then fifteen year-old daughter kept telling me.

This puzzled me.

Me, not understand kids?! Me? Had I not devoted my entire life to preventing problems among young people? I even wrote a book about it! Had I not run many parenting courses, and trained many parenting instructors? More important, did I not have what I considered to be a good relationship with my own daughter?

"Jaime, what do you mean by that?" I asked.

"You just don't."

Not overly helpful! But I did want to understand. My daughter could not articulate it. She had only a vague feeling.

I did see Jaime taking less and less responsibility. If anything went wrong she would always blame someone or something else. She always had an excuse. She began to treat her mother with contempt. We also saw Jaime becoming increasingly unhappy. This concerned us deeply, for we seemed powerless to do anything about it.

Then, one day, Jaime had a breakthrough. She had been too close to see it.

It began the night she stayed over at a friend's house, after her friend had attended a huge party and had not bothered to inform her parents. Jaime watched the mother confront her friend about misrepresenting her whereabouts and not coming home when expected. The mother said they had given her a certain amount of trust and freedom. It was a big deal to let a fourteen-year-old go to a party, and she should have shown her parents more respect.

Jaime watched her friend completely shut her mother out, not listening to anything she said. Jaime could relate. Her friend had heard her mother say such things a hundred times, and it had stopped registering. Instead of taking in its truth her friend got snotty and angry and yelled, "You don't understand anything!"

It looked all too familiar. Observing it from a distance, not caught up in the emotions, not feeling threatened, Jaime realized that she too had a tendency to react in the same way whenever a power figure loomed over her. To Jaime, her friend's mother made a lot of sense. *Trust* was at stake! Her friend's parents needed to know what her friend was up to. How else would they know whether to stay up until she had arrived home safely, whether she had stayed over at someone's house, or whether she'd been raped and was lying somewhere in a gutter.

Jaime could relate to the feeling. Whenever her own parents got on her case about anything, rather than listen she would be scrambling, trying to figure out what she could say to protect herself, blocking out the words, saying over and over to herself, "This is so stupid! This is so stupid!"

Jaime thought, "It must be something about the way all parents come across: 'This-is-the-way-it's-going-to-be-and-if-it's-not-here's-what-will-happen.' But in the end kids make their own decisions anyway, no matter what their parents say."

The next day, at our own house, Jaime's mother, Judy, came in exhausted from a hard day's work to find that Jaime had a lot of friends over and had basically trashed the house.

"Jaime, I can't believe you could do this!" Judy snapped.

2

Jaime felt herself tuning out from her mother as her friend had. She could pick up the slightest edge in a tone of voice miles away—long before her mother even noticed it herself. Jaime's antennae were way up. She would be waiting to pounce whenever she heard a tone change, which invariably resulted in the butting of heads and a fight.

No one veered from their positions. In the middle of the argument, it occurred to Judy that they were having a power struggle; that Jaime was trying to assert her power and Judy's own power was holding it back. She attempted to express this to Jaime, but Jaime didn't hear it as intended.

So frustrated and red-faced it looked like she would burst, Jaime yelled, "I hate you! I hate you! I love you because you're my mother, but I hate you!"

Judy was at wit's end.

"It's not like it was!" Jaime cried. "You don't hold me any more and tell me you love me like you used to. You're just on my case. You just come in and say how disappointed you are in me, how I let you down. I can't live up to your expectations of me!"

"What do you want me to do?" Judy replied. "Is it too much to expect for you not to add to my burden when I come home?"

At this point Jaime grabbed her head and let out a scream. "AAAUUUGHHH! I can't stand it anymore!"

I was sitting on the other side of the room watching all this. (I do not mean to suggest that I came riding in on a white horse here; Judy has bailed me out on many an occasion.) However, as I was not personally involved in the conversation—as detached as Jaime had been with her friend—I was not the one feeling threatened, causing my guard to be up. So while Judy saw this as an issue of power, I heard something else.

3

"Wait," I said, "the point isn't power. The point is love. Jaime is saying that we could tell her to do anything, so long as we say it with love and understanding."

Jaime nodded through her tears. No matter what we told her it could be communicated in a nonaccusatory way—in a loving way. I realized that if love isn't being felt in the moment, only then do issues of power come into play.

Judy then had a breakthrough. "Oh, you mean it's not what I say, it's how I say it?"

We could say, "Jaime, honey, would you mind picking this up please," instead of "How could you do this!" and have her take it as a personal affront.

Jaime said, "Even when you're mad—especially around little things, like if you leave your light on, it should be, like, 'Jaime, honey, you left your light on,' or saying it with a smile on your face. Things get across to kids better that way. Because it doesn't really matter in the whole scheme of things. It can bug you, but it can bug you in a happy way, as opposed to, 'Why don't you ever do that right!'"

My God, she is right! She is so right!

It's the key to it all.

I was even writing about it, and I didn't see it under my nose. I understood it on an intellectual level but had not connected it in my heart. Of course I knew this, but knowing it intellectually means nothing.

Our daughter helped us see that this is the only thing that really counts in parenting. It's the cake; everything else is the icing. **What our kids feel from us in the moment is the only thing that really matters.**

This goes for our own kids, as well as the kids we work with or teach.

It must go beyond intellectual understanding—to the heart.

We can see it in those who work best with kids; we can see it in the teachers that students love. Such individuals naturally create a loving, supportive, lighthearted feeling. Teenagers, children, feel it from them. This is why they are so good with kids and help them have breakthroughs in understandings.

In a sense it does not even matter what we say. It's what our children feel coming out of us toward them from our hearts.

Every day I thank my lucky stars for this breakthrough. At ages sixteen and seventeen Jaime was an absolute delight to be around, to have around. We developed the most wonderful, warm, loving relationship. By her senior year people kept commenting to us about how happy and self-assured she always seemed to be.

In sum, here is the essence of what is being said: **If we want our children to both respond to us well and live a life of well-being, they must live in a loving feeling. The number one-most-important-by-far-bar-none thing that we can do for our children is to create a loving, supportive, caring, respectful, lighthearted environment.** And we don't need to know any parenting techniques to do it.

Of course we know this! This is not new news. But there is one catch: A loving environment is a moment-to-moment thing.

What?

The feeling we have at the time is the environment that the child is living in at that moment.

When we feel angry, our children are living in an angry environment. When we feel scared, our children are living in a fearful environment. When we feel disappointed our children are living in an environment of, "I-can't-live-up-to-their-expectations." No matter what we try to communicate to them at those times the feeling we have inside us is what they pick up, the environment that surrounds them at that moment. If we are fearful or anxious or worried or angry or disappointed or any number of emotions, our children are not living in a loving, caring, supportive, environment at those times—even if we generally show love to our children and tell them many times a day that we love them. If we think they are, we are kidding ourselves.

LOVE IN THE MOMENT

So what does this suggest we do?

Another story may help illustrate this. A few years before I realized this I listened to a tape about relationships, based on this same approach, called "Can Love Survive Commitment," by Darlene and Charles Stewart. Toward the end of the tape Darlene began to describe the very difficult time they had been having with their teenage son who was getting into a lot of trouble. She said they had been trying to change him, trying to get him to do what was right—to no avail. One day it struck her. She said to herself [something like], "I decided I was going to stop trying to change him, I was just going to love him—even if I have to bring him cookies in jail."

The "cookies in jail" line got to me. It struck me as a completely wild, profound, idea.

Darlene decided to back off trying to make him right. She simply went out of her way to show him love. Their relationship improved enormously. Remarkably, her son's troubling behaviors began to diminish.

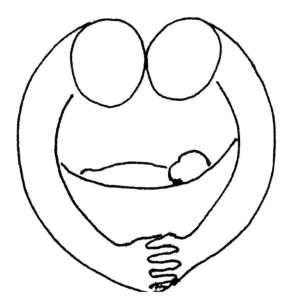

Despite how it affected me at the time I heard it, and how it had helped me at the time to deal with my son, I had all but forgotten about it until this incident with my daughter. Now it came roaring back. I decided on the spot that I would commit to dropping my thoughts of disappointment about what she was, or was not, doing right. Before I communicated anything to her I decided to watch what was in my heart and be sure I sent out love. I decided to go out of my way to create that loving environment around her at every moment I could, certainly every moment I wanted to communicate anything to her. Judy ended up doing the same.

It worked! We became much closer and, miraculously, Jaime became more helpful. When we backed off, she responded.

The irony did not go unnoticed. The more we were on her case, the less it worked. The less we were on her case, the more it worked.

Everyone responds to love, respect, caring, support, lightheartedness. Everyone responds when there is a good feeling in a relationship.

II. INNATE HEALTH AND COMMON SENSE

In raising children, why would building a loving, caring, supportive, lighthearted atmosphere work?

To answer this we begin with an important principle: **The way we see our children will determine how successful we will be in raising them.**

Read that again.

What we see is what we get.

If we see someone as lovable we tend to treat that person as lovable. When we treat someone in a lovable way that person tends to respond in a more lovable way. If we see someone as mean and rotten we tend to treat that person as if s/he is. People feel the way we treat them and respond accordingly.

Each of us can see our children in any way we want. We decide.

One healthy way to see our children lies in seeing a basic principle of human nature. **Our children are all born in a state of pure mental health and well-being that naturally allows them to function in a healthy way.**

If you don't believe this, take a close look at little babies. Until the "real world" starts impinging on their senses in a way that makes them feel uncomfortable they are pure joy and pure wonder. Pure love. Pure innocence. A perfect little package. No insecure thoughts.

Think of the feeling you had in your heart the first time you saw your newborn. What most of us feel for that precious little infant in that moment is what they are naturally born with. This pure joy and wonder is part of their spirit. It's what makes them what they are. It stands apart from any physical infirmities they may bring with them into the world (including in their brains). It lies beyond all that. It is the human spirit, and that spirit is perfection. It is inside them and never goes away. Never–for any of us!

The human spirit is always glowing inside people, even when it no longer looks like they have it. Given the way our kids behave sometimes we may think it disappears, but the following three chapters will show why kids behave in problematic ways. For now, all we need to know is, no matter what painful, difficult, or traumatic experiences we go through, no matter what kinds of thoughts we develop about ourselves, no matter how much we forget that we have it, we still have this natural, healthy state inside us, and we always have access to it. So do our children.

Think of this innate health as the seed of a flower. The seed contains within it all the information it ever needs to grow into a healthy flower. All we have to do is put it in the right environment—the right moisture, sunlight, warmth, soil—and it will grow into a flower on its own. The seed is naturally programmed that way. The same is true naturally in our children. Put children in a loving, warm, caring, nurturing, lighthearted environment, and they will blossom and flourish, because it draws out what they already have within them.

MOVING TOWARD HEALTH

Like the trees in the forest that naturally gravitate toward the light, our children have a natural tendency to move toward their mental health, toward happiness, toward good feelings about themselves, toward peace of mind, toward healthy, productive relationships.

This means that we need to recognize this in our kids. **We need to see that each of our children** (and this includes us because we were all children once) **is born with this natural state of mental health, happiness, self-esteem, and with the ability to act with wisdom and common sense, to see what's in their best interests, and to do what's best for themselves and others. It's a God-given, innate, completely natural capacity. We need to have faith and trust that it is there, no matter how our kids are behaving.**

No child is born bad. Kids are healthier than we think. They are born with everything they need to have a happy, healthy life.

How do we know this is true?

It cannot be proven.

What if some parents do not believe that their children have innate health? What if it is too big a leap of faith? Might those parents be able to accept that that their children at least have the capability to act in healthy ways? If we look closely at people we can observe that even the most troubling or troubled people have moments when they act healthier than at other times. This means that they have this capacity within them. Yet, what if even this statement is too great a leap for some parents? Even if they didn't believe it, if these parents were to treat their children *as if* they had the capacity to attain their health at any moment, they would be far better off, because their children would respond accordingly.

Those who truly see the health in people can feel it. They know that all people, no matter how terribly they act, have goodness inside them. They know that no one is born insecure, or destructive or disruptive, or born with bad thoughts of others. They know that we have to learn and acquire these. They know that when they see their children or anyone act out, it means that person is only lost, that they've lost their bearings or their perspective. They have simply lost touch with the health or wisdom inside them. If our children become lost—and this seems to happen to all children from time to time—our job becomes to help them find it again. Our job is to help draw out their health. No, we cannot prove the existence of innate health. All we know is that those who believe in it and treat their children and others as if they have these internal qualities usually get better results than those who do not.

In sum, for practical reasons if nothing else, even if we cannot find it in our hearts to accept that our children have innate health and wisdom, we can act toward them as if they do. Simply by doing that, we will find ourselves on the right path to productive and satisfying parenting—for what we see is what we get.

DRAWING OUT HEALTH

This answers why it works to establish a warm, loving, caring, lighthearted environment. Simply put, it draws out what is already inside. Children respond better in this kind of atmosphere because they gravitate to their true nature.

It would not be difficult to create this kind of climate if we could only carry around in our hearts the same beautiful feelings for our children that we experienced when they were first born, or when as little beings they had just done something exceptionally cute and endearing. It would be the most natural thing in the world.

Here are two pieces of good news:

1. That beautiful feeling for our children—carried in our hearts and communicated to them through our spirit—can overcome any lack of knowledge of specific parenting skills;

2. We already have that feeling for our children—it's already there. It is part of the package of health inside us.

The problem is, when we're caught up in the emotions of the moment, we forget. If our child has been defying us over time it is especially hard to remember that feeling. Yet, the initial, beautiful feeling never goes away—even when our kids are acting out or not doing what they should. This feeling is an inherent part of us. It may be buried but it is never gone.

How do we know this?

Did you ever notice that when you get upset or angry, once that upset or anger fades and the problem is resolved, the good feeling eventually comes back? Or, if a bad feeling has built over time (due to serious problems), every once in a while when your guard is down, or when your child's is down, you can feel that good feeling slip through even when you aren't expecting it, if only for a moment. And during that moment, if only fleeting, you glimpse the kind of relationship you want with your children. That we can experience it even for a moment means we have that capacity inside us. All we have to do is learn how to find it and have it become our predominant feeling when dealing with our children.

SUMMARY

To summarize, if we really pay attention to what this means and listen to our own common sense, we realize a few things:

1. Those warm, beautiful, loving feelings for our children are always there; they've just been covered up by extraneous thoughts.

2. We can access those feelings—because from time to time we do.

3. When we do, we have a nice relationship—even if it lasts only a short time.

4. The more we access those warm feelings, the better our relationship will be.

How can we find that warm, good feeling when we don't feel that feeling?

The odd thing is, to find it we do not need to do anything. Remember, we already have that feeling lying deep within our hearts, so all we have to do is get out of its way. We need to get out of our own way to allow what is naturally inside us to rise to the surface. We need only to get the thoughts out of the way that are keeping us from feeling it.

The next chapter will tell us how to accomplish this. Before we get there, however, what is this chapter suggesting?

Since children are already pure love, they will respond best when we give them love, caring attention and understanding. Since they are already naturally full of joy and wonder (which is the natural capacity to reach out and learn), we want to interfere with that feeling as little as possible. Since little babies' thoughts are uncontaminated, we want to do our best not to contaminate them with our own craziness [See Chapter III].

A Miami family therapist perhaps puts it best: "Where parents go wrong is they look at their children and see something incomplete, and they feel like they have to fix it. But it's impossible to complete something that is already perfectly complete. When parents begin to see that they're pretty nice people, and have something nice to give, and relax a little, and get a nice feeling back, they then look at the child and see a different person. They see a child that has the capacity to grow, to learn, to give love, to behave well. Kids, like all human beings, are geared to behaving well, to learning naturally. If the parent is able to calm down, that parent can see the child's potential and provide a safe, non judgmental, respectful, loving feeling in the home to bring it out in them. Parents are guides. **Rather than see the incomplete, see that there is nothing wrong with our children except our own perceptions. See them with a sense of wonder. See them as a limitless, infinite capacity to grow."**

Remember: We do not have to do anything to make our children become good kids. They already are.

III. WE ARE WHAT WE THINK

Judy and I agreed to take in a temporary foster child, twelve years old. Jennifer [her name has been changed] and her mother had had a terrible fight. Allegedly Jen had been beaten badly. We heard that her mother's boyfriend had been abusing Jen. Encouraged by her thirteen year old boyfriend, Jen called the state department of social services and was temporarily removed from her home. She'd been virtually living on the streets.

It did not take us long to learn that Jen had developed some bad habits. We caught her in a lie. Then another. Then another. She stole some money to support her cigarette addiction. She manipulated everyone around her to get what she wanted. When Judy caught her in the lies and pointed them out to her Jen became angry. "You know too many people around here," she snapped.

Her entire life seemed to consist of lying, cheating, stealing, manipulating.

Jen wanted to be with her real father. Her father wanted her too yet was afraid to take her in because he was also trying to gain custody of his three younger children. He also knew that, given Jen's propensity for being on the streets, he didn't have the parenting skills to keep Jen under control. In our presence he kindly lectured her about his fears and how she would have to give him assurance that he could take her in without problems. Jen promised to be responsible.

It took only a day for us to catch her in another lie— something about needing to go to a friend's house to do a special school project "on Hebrews." When we checked, we discovered that the school had never heard of this project. Next, Jen invited her mother over to our house, despite that the state forbade her to see her mother except in their offices under their supervision. Jen then ran out on our daughter Jaime who was looking after her when we were out having a teacher conference about Jaime's progress.

The next day Jen was scheduled to go to court to learn where she would be placed. For some reason I woke up in the middle of the night feeling incredible clarity about Jen's problem:

Nothing, absolutely nothing, was wrong with Jen, except for her thinking.

Jennifer's thinking was off kilter. In other words, but for her thinking, she would be a perfectly normal functioning twelve year old—a fine kid. Destructive conditions at home may have caused her thinking to be skewed, but the only damaged part of Jen was her thinking process, and that could always change. I saw it so clearly!

Yet, nothing in the entire social services system was designed to help Jen or any other young people understand how their thinking was getting them into trouble, so it could change.

THOUGHT IS THE KEY

If not for their thinking, all teenagers would be wonderful human beings. Something lies beyond their presenting behavior. Behind all behavior problems lies a certain type of thinking.

Remember, hidden beneath the off-kilter thinking that makes people feel bad and gets them into trouble lies that glowing ember of the pure love, goodness and health that they brought with them into the world. They then learned their way away from it.

18

The only thing keeping them from seeing and being in touch with their beautiful, inner, healthy, loving energy deep inside them is their thinking—no matter how bad or problematic their behavior.[*]

CHILDREN ARE ALWAYS DOING THEIR BEST

What we see of our children's behavior is the way they have learned to respond to life. How they think has a lot to do with how they were treated and what they were told, and what they took in as they were growing up—and now they are just trying to respond in the best way they know how. They don't know how to respond in any other way. **They're doing the best they know how at the time, given the way they see things. In that sense they are innocent.** Jen was innocent. She didn't know what else to do; she didn't know how else to respond.

When Judy and I were caught up in Jaime's antics [Chapter I] and didn't know how to respond well, we too were innocent because we didn't see any other way at the time. Jaime was innocent because she didn't know any other way at that time. Now she does, so she acts completely differently. So do we.

So, besides going out of our way to show Jaime love, we also started to help Jaime take a look at her thinking and how it was affecting her. She saw it! This changed the entire tenor of our relationship.

---

[*]Note: I know some would argue that in some cases physical problems or chemical imbalances or A.D.H.D and other disorders cause some kids to behave badly, and I do not dispute this. It is also possible, however, that the thinking could have preceded the imbalance or disorder, or that people's thinking stands between the imbalance or disorder and the behavior, causing it to be manifested in different ways.

Alas, with Jen we did not have time to put this into practice. Sadly, she was placed in a permanent foster home.

Suppose all parents understood not only how to draw out the innate health in their children, but also how to help their children see how their own thinking is creating what they experience from life. As this chapter proceeds, you will be able to see more what this means, but from this new vantage point, their thoughts, feelings and behaviors would change. They would see with new eyes. Instead, many of us find ourselves troubled by our children's behavior, unable to find the feeling in our hearts that we need to help our children see their thinking.

What can we do when we're in this position? We first need to understand what makes kids behave as they do.

Our understanding of why children behave the way they do (and why we behave the way we do) will determine our effectiveness and satisfaction in dealing with them.

WHY KIDS BEHAVE AS THEY DO

If we accept the principle from the last chapter that children are not born insecure or with spiteful or troubled behavior, where do they get it? If children have wisdom and common sense inside them, why don't they often use it?

Here's why: From the moment we're born we start forgetting that we have it. We begin to have experiences. We form thoughts about those experiences. Our parents tell us things, and we form thoughts about what our parents tell us. This process is a necessary part of life. We develop a way of thinking to help us make sense out of the world.

Such thinking causes us to see ourselves in certain ways. Some thoughts can make us feel insecure. Some can make us afraid. Some thoughts can make us judgmental of others. Some can make us feel bad. Some can make us angry. Some thoughts can make us feel that we have to behave in certain ways to maintain what we have learned to think about ourselves. Many of these thoughts take us away from our natural state of well-being and self-esteem. Many thoughts get so loud in our heads that we can no longer hear our inner wisdom and common sense.

In short, innocently, we have begun to think ourselves away from our health.

No one does this intentionally. It just seems to happen to all of us as we live and grow.

One of the secrets to whether we will raise children in a healthy, productive, satisfying, joyful way—and one of the secrets to our own happiness and peace of mind—is to understand that if we could somehow get those unproductive thoughts out of the way, the inner, natural state will automatically rise to the surface.

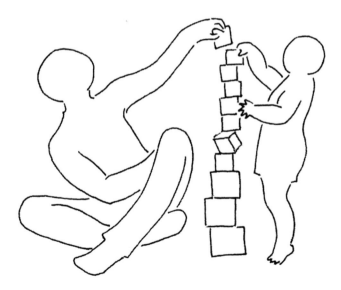

21

Dr. Roger Mills likens it to holding a cork under water. The cork is buoyant, so it is always trying to rise to the surface. As our hand is the only thing keeping the cork down, so our thoughts are the only things keeping our innate health and wisdom down. This implies that we don't have to *do* anything except get out of our own way. All we have to do is let go of the cork and it will naturally rise on its own. All we have to do is let go of, dismiss, forget about, or discredit the thoughts that are keeping those natural, inner feelings submerged.

If this concept seems vague or impractical or too simple or too complex or off the subject of raising kids at this point, fear not. Concern is only another of those thoughts that can get in the way. As the book unfolds so will your understanding of how this works and how it is possible to apply this in day-to-day situations. What we are talking about here is the foundation for everything that follows.

Children act out or act troubled because the thinking they have learned and taken on has made them lose touch with their natural state of well-being and common sense. This thinking has made it appear to them that they should act exactly as they are. In other words, given what they believe and how the world looks to them at that moment, they have no other choice but to feel and act that way. This is why they are always doing the best they know at the time.

What, then, does this suggest we do?

When we step back and look at it, what we need to do is common sense. If our children have natural goodness and the personal resources they need already inside them, and if they also have certain thoughts that create insecurities that lead them to act in troubling ways, two things need to happen:

1. We can help them tap into their inner, natural state so they can let their own wisdom and common sense guide them;

2. We can help them understand how not to let their negative or insecure thoughts get in their way.

To accomplish these would take us 90% along the road to successful parenting.

CREATING INSECURE THINKING

When our children are young, if we yell at them and put them down or nag them and criticize them and tell them they're not okay, we are inadvertently teaching them to have insecure thoughts about themselves. They then become those thoughts.

When schools tell kids that they won't fit in, or they won't do well, or they will have trouble learning, or that they're troublemakers, if young people believe it they will think it themselves; then they will think that is what they are worth. This will keep them looking outside themselves for the answer about what they are.

This leads to an insecure set of beliefs. If parents are always telling a kid that he's stupid, and then something happens to fit into those beliefs, such as getting an "F" on a test, he may think something like, "They must be right, I am stupid." Those beliefs get reinforced. Once those beliefs are entrenched and become a pattern, then even when something comes along that contradicts it, such as getting an "A" the kid may think something like, "Oh, that was just a fluke," and write it off. So once those beliefs are locked in, whatever comes along confirms and validates them. No matter what comes along, those kids will think they are stupid and act as if they really are. The world then reacts to them accordingly which, in turn, reinforces it. A vicious downward thinking cycle develops. This is what moves children and other people away from their natural state.

Don't forget, we parents have also picked up such beliefs. Where did we get them from? From our parents! Then without being aware of it we pass them along to our children. For example, if your mother was a worrier, you likely picked up this worry and are passing it along like a baton in a relay race. Probably you're not passing it along in the exact way, but in some way you are. It then gets programmed into our children's brains, as it was inadvertently programmed into ours.

Dr. George Pransky says that our children pick up "as if worlds" from us. This means we begin to go through life *as if* certain things about life are most important. If our parents inadvertently taught us by their actions that we should go through life *as if* money is important, we begin to see everything we encounter in life in terms of money.

When my son was a freshman in college and about to go to his first prom, he said to his mother that he couldn't believe how expensive it was to rent the tux and pay for admission. Judy said, "Dave, since when did you get so concerned about money? Where did you get that from?" Without batting an eyelash, he said, "From dad!"

Ugh! A humbling moment.

Somewhere along the line I began to see life as if money was enormously important. I never realized how much it was on my mind. I would go out of my way not to spend money on myself. I would cringe when I thought something was too expensive. It would unknowingly affect the way I was feeling. Then I graciously passed it along to my son.

Is it a coincidence that my mother prides herself on being frugal?

Innocently we pick up such things from our parents. We might even take them the wrong way—in a way unintended, but they become our own.

Yet, other people do not think of money that way. They might go through life as if power or prestige were the all-important thing in life—or a million other things that a million other people *think* are *the way it really is.*

Of course, I picked up other things too. To my folks, "family" is the most important thing in the world, so I also have come to see the world in terms of the importance of family. This sounds good—until I try to shove family obligations down my kids' throats, no matter what is going on with them at the time.

Judy does not understand "time." In her family of origin people went about their business until they finished whatever they were doing, so they were rarely on time for things. I don't even start counting that Judy is late until after an hour has passed. That she is continually late drives our kids crazy. Of course, our kids say they will never do that to their kids, and they take pride in not being that way themselves. But both of them procrastinate until the very last moment to do what they need to do, so they are continually in a mad, hurried, harried, frustrated dash to get somewhere on time. This reflects how insidious this all is.

Another parent will imply that we should go through life as if not backing down from anyone is important. That kid will likely end up in a lot of fights.

Another parent will say that life is all about trusting people. This sounds good—until that kid ends up trusting everyone to the point of being taken advantage of.

For other parents life is all about hard work. This sounds good too—until some become workaholics. For others life is all about survival—doing anything you need to do to survive. We could go on and on.

We parents might ask ourselves what we picked up from our parents that we might be inadvertently passing along to our children. Yet, for every one we know about, there is at least another that we have no idea we're also carrying with us and passing along. We could call this a "blind spot." We all have them. Our partners or friends or close work associates could probably tell us what they are. We could tell them theirs, but we often can't see our own. They are hidden from us, but we still think them unknowingly.

The importance of this for raising our children cannot be overstated. This is how our children's programmed thinking develops. **Out of this habitual, programmed thinking they then see the world, and out of how they see the world they think, feel and act.**

COLORING OUR WORLDS

George Pransky tells a story of how he and his wife were once camping in the woods with another couple. The guy, who is usually very laid back, demanded that they hurry up and get wood for the fire. George couldn't figure out why his friend was acting as if there was such a rush, but he went along with him. George wanted to stop and see some of the beautiful scenery in the great Northwest, but his friend told him there wasn't time, and they had to quickly get the wood and get it back to the campsite. When they arrived back at the campsite their partners were lying down relaxing and reading, and his friend tried to hurry everyone up to get the campfire going. His wife said, "I'm really not ready to move just yet." Then she looked up at him and asked, "Why are you wearing your sunglasses?" He put his hand to his eyes and bumped them, then took them off and said, "Woah, it's early!"

He thought it was getting dark, and because it was late they'd better quickly snap to it and get the fire going. The sunglasses that he did not know he was wearing colored the way he saw everything, which in turn colored the way he felt, which in turn colored the way he acted.

This is what happens to us all the time. This is what happens with our kids. We are all looking out of different colored lenses and acting as if what we are seeing is the way life really is.

Any of us who have ever put on a pair of strangely colored sunglasses at first sees the world looking very strange. But if we keep them on for a long time we begin to get used to them and everything begins to look "normal." This is what happens with our programmed thinking..

Everyone is seeing the world through a different colored pair of lenses that they don't know they have on. Yet they think what they're seeing is the way it really is. And for everyone it is different. This explains why there are so many fights and arguments and disagreements. Everyone is living in a separate world, a separate reality, that they each think is right.

So are our kids. Our kids live in separate worlds from us. They therefore think differently, feel differently, and act differently than we do. Just as we think our world is right, they think theirs is right. No wonder we have so many conflicts!

We and our children may have some similarities in our ways of thinking, but we still have had different experiences, and we still all interpret those experiences very differently.

WHAT TO DO

What does this suggest about dealing with our kids?

First, we want to be a little careful about how seriously we take our own thinking. If we paid close attention we could tell when a programmed pattern rears its head. It sounds all too familiar. If we know this, we may want to be a little more careful about what we lay on our kids, because it comes from our own "reality" of what we think is important.

Second, we want to understand that when we react to children in a negative way that becomes a pattern, the children pick it up for themselves as a negative thinking pattern. They then act out of those patterns. So if we want kids who behave well, we have to watch how we think and behave.

One might ask, if we go out of our way not to program in negativity, what do the children have left? What they have left is the natural good feelings about themselves. If we do not inject negativity, the natural good rises to the surface. **Negative thoughts are the only thing keeping down the naturally positive feelings.**

Since no one is perfect—certainly including this author/parent—the less we treat our kids in ways that breed negative or unhealthy or destructive or problematic thoughts, the better off we will be in raising our children, because the less they will have a tendency to act out of those kinds of habitual, programmed thoughts.

We must be mindful that our children are acting based on their thinking, and much of their thinking stems from what they have been innocently exposed to and learned. We and our children are both innocently caught up in the web through which we each now see.

The more we can watch our children in their thought patterns, and watch ourselves in our thought patterns, and not take either too seriously because it is only real to each of us, the better off we will be.

Another way to see this is, the only thing we have to do to experience that pure love for our children is to drop our thoughts of bother about what our kids are or are not doing. In other words, but for our bothered or other distracted thoughts we would be experiencing naturally pure feelings of love. If you are having trouble conceiving how it could be possible to drop thoughts of bother when you're bothered, picture what would happen to these thoughts if you were yelling at your daughter and suddenly she fainted, or if you found out that your son only had a week to live. Suddenly, leaving clothes scattered around the house wouldn't mean so much. We only have thoughts of bother or upset when we're not thinking about something else.

What can we do? We have two good choices: 1) We could see ourselves being bothered and know it is not serving us well. This distance (watching ourselves instead of being caught up in it) often takes the power out of our bother. 2) Even better, we can realize that our feelings of bother simply can and will change with another thought, and therefore we don't have to consider our bother as "reality," and we can take it less seriously. More on this in the next chapter.

The way we function as parents depends on our thoughts at the time. The way our children behave toward us and the world depends on whatever they are thinking at the time. Some of our thoughts compel us to act in certain ways, and to react in certain ways to what our children do.

IV. STATES OF MIND – MOODS

I come home from a hard day's work. I'm tired. I'm crabby. I'm snappy. I see that Jaime has once again dropped her books and jacket and boots and everything else she owns right in front of the door. I grumble to myself, "This girl has learned nothing! She's doing it to me again! I've been totally incapable of teaching her responsibility." I spot her upstairs and yell, "Jaime, how many times do I have to tell you to get this crap out of here!" She yaps back and makes another excuse.

It's the weekend. I wake up calm and relaxed, in good spirits. I walk downstairs and notice that Jaime has again left her stuff in the hallway. I smile. When I see her I say cheerfully, "Hey Jaim's, how about moving your stuff?" She says, "Okay dad, sorry," and picks it up.

Same books, same coat, same hallway; different moods, different view, different outcomes.

In a low mood, what she did speaks to the very heart of my capability as a parent and to her incapability as a kid. In a good mood it's water off a duck's back.

MOODS AFFECT ACTION

Being effective and successful as a parent has more to do with a parent's state of mind than whether the parent knows parenting techniques.

When parents are upset or in low moods they tend to forget the techniques they know. At such times, even if they had they had the presence of mind to use the techniques, the techniques will not necessarily come out right. A bad feeling seeps through and negates their usefulness because kids react more to the feeling.

In a good mood when spirits are high, at those times the parent's mood will override naturally the need for techniques.

More than techniques parents need an understanding of moods and their effect on one's parenting at any given time.

Children respond better when we deal with them from a responsive, secure frame of mind.

At any given moment every human being is in one of two states of mind: a secure, responsive state, or an insecure, reactive state. Of course there are many varying degrees, but there also seems to be a line that, once crossed, puts us in one state or the other.

We all know what both states feel like. We have all visited both. All the time we go up and down and back and forth between these states. We can tell the difference. In the reactive state we tend to act out of fear and insecurity. We seem to have a lot of knee-jerk reactions. We feel threatened. In the responsive state we tend to act out of security and out of our own sense of what is best. We keep our bearings.

Moods are part of the human condition. We look out at the world from our various moods and what we see changes. We react to our children according the mood we are in at the time. Remember, our moods go up and down all the time like the ocean has tides. When up we're relaxed, we're lighthearted, we listen more. When down, we see those around us in a negative way; we overreact.

DIFFERENT MOODS, DIFFERENT PEOPLE

A little-realized fact is that we are completely different people in low, reactive moods than in high, responsive moods. We are Dr. Jeckyl and Mr. Hyde. If someone met you for the first time when you were in a low mood, and someone else met you for the first time when you were in a high mood, and the two people then got together and described to each other what you were like, they would each think they were talking about two completely different people.

When we act out of one state, as opposed to the other, what we say and do is completely different; the results are completely different.

The state of mind we are in when interacting with our children at any given time will determine how effectively we will deal with them.

Since we naturally go in and out of each of these states—up and down in our many moods—and since we can't do all that much about being in any mood at any given time, the key becomes how we act when in each of those states. From which state of mind would we rather talk, act, or make decisions?

MOOD AWARENESS

The first step is simply to be aware of which state of mind we are in at any given time.

We can tell which state we're in by how we feel. If we're feeling great, we're in the secure, responsive state; when we are feeling lousy or low or angry or frantic or fearful we have slid into the insecure, reactive state. Noticing how we feel when we're about to confront or talk to our kids provides our first signal about how to proceed.

In a negative, reactive state, even the smallest problem seems large. It is difficult to see solutions. In the secure, responsive state, problems don't look so overwhelming. We see the way out. Things look hopeful. Problems seem more manageable. In fact, some problems that loomed large in a negative, reactive state don't even look like problems from a more positive state. Which is "reality?"

Our kids also jump back and forth between these two states every day, sometimes many times a day.

The best time to deal with our kids, then, especially in trying to help them learn something, is when we're both in positive, open, responsive states. In negative, reactive moods we are simply not going to come across well. Our kids will react by getting a little frightened or insecure and resist what we say. In a low state, they are automatically closed to whatever anyone tries to tell them.

MOOD THINKING AND ACTION

So what do we do when we're in a low state and must get something across to our kids?

The best thing to do in an insecure, reactive state or low mood is nothing, or as little as we can possibly get away with.

All we have to do is wait it out. If we are in a low mood, our mood is guaranteed to rise, eventually. (If we are in a high mood, our mood will drop, eventually.) Very few situations are so urgent that they must be dealt with at that moment. In most cases we have about eighteen years to be with our kids, to help them learn from us. How much time will we lose if we wait out a low mood before acting? We nearly always have a second chance. Will we take it?

Needless to say, if a child is in danger or if an emergency arises, it doesn't matter what mood we are in; of course the danger at the moment must always be dealt with first. But **when neither danger nor an emergency is present, if we are in a low state and need to teach them something about their behavior, we need to stop, bite our tongues, step back for a while, and regain**

perspective—for as long as it takes—until we feel a healthier state of mind kick in. Then we can deal with it.

Likewise, if our kids are in low moods, they first need to calm down enough to hear it, so they may need to be separated for a while until they regain their bearings. When spirits have risen on both sides, we can then get together and talk from a more productive perspective.

Put simply, we are wasting our time and energy trying to deal with our children when either of us is in a low state. Plus, the more we do it, the more it harms the relationship.

If we do not have good feelings, or if we are overwrought or wound up about something, or if we are thinking thoughts about how bad or how difficult our kids are, those are the worst times to deal with our children. That is simply low-mood thinking. **Our thinking and our moods are essentially one and the same; our thinking is tied up with our moods. Low moods equal low-quality thoughts.** When feeling low or frantic or angry, etc. we simply need to take the space to clear our heads in whatever way it works for us. When caught up in our emotions, we're the ones who need the "time out!"

Some of us may have to completely remove ourselves from the situation a while until we feel more calm and able to have thoughts that come from that calmer place inside us. Some of us may have to remove our child for a while until s/he calms down. Some of us may have to wait out an extended bad mood. Some may have to count to ten. Whatever it takes is different for each individual. To deal constructively, however, we must deal with the child when both of us are in a calm, rational frame of mind.

Sometimes we may have to tell our child that we're too upset to deal with something just then. Sometimes we may have to say something like, "It looks like you need to calm down some before we talk about this, so we'll talk about it later."

MAKING ADJUSTMENTS

The problem, of course, is that in low moods we feel most compelled to say or do something. However, if we recognize how destructive this can be, this recognition might be enough to hold our tongues or fists. **In low moods we must make adjustments.** The adjustment is to back off and wait.

In summary, what do we do when we cannot seem to find that responsive state of mind, or find that loving, caring, warm feeling for our child in the moment?

1. **The first thing we need to do is recognize when we are in an insecure, reactive state or in a low mood.**
This is not so difficult to recognize once we begin to pay attention to how we are feeling. Remember, our feelings always tell us which state we are in at any given

time. All we have to do is be aware. Remember too, what we are feeling is the climate we're creating at the moment.

2. **If our feeling tells us that we are in a secure, responsive state, it serves as a signal—a green light—that it is okay to go ahead and act, because at that time we can pretty much trust whatever naturally comes up to deal with a situation.** [More on this in Chapter VI.]

3. **If our feeling tells us that we are in a low, reactive mood, it serves as a signal—a red light—to stop and move into "damage control."** In this state it is best not to try to teach anything to our children or to discipline them at that moment, and it is best to clear our heads and get ourselves back on track.

If we are unsure of our feeling, it serves as a yellow light—slow down and proceed with caution.

If we are upset and then our child does something that upsets us even more, we still need to understand that any action we take at that time will make the child feel more insecure. This is because we are feeling insecure, and when our insecure buttons are pushed we have more of a tendency to want to take control and to take personally what the child has done. From that insecure state, we will then worsen the child's insecurity.

Backing off and clearing our heads gets us back on track. Sometimes going off by ourselves, or saying we don't want to be disturbed for a while, or doing something nice for ourselves—or anything that gets our heads clear—will help us then get back with our children in a good frame of mind.

Sometimes this is easier said than done. If a single parent, for example, has a screaming little kid on her hands, has no relatives in the vicinity to help bail her out, doesn't have the money to hire a babysitter for an hour or two, has a one-room apartment, and there's a blizzard outside so she can't take the kid out for a walk, it can be awfully difficult.

However, even during those times, we can pay attention to our feeling and know it means we will not be reacting well at that moment and that it will eventually pass. If we can hold ourselves together long enough to make sure the kid is all right and has his biological needs tended to and is safe, if the kid still insists on screaming, we can reassure him that we need to be by ourselves for a little while but that we'll be back, and then we might put on headphones, or stick cotton in our ears and read a good book, or take a hot bath, or do whatever it takes to calm ourselves so we can go back to him in a good frame of mind.

This does not mean to ignore or neglect the child! At those times we must still keep alert enough to prevent any disasters. All this means is, within the parameters of safety, do as little as we can possibly get away with, and do something nice to improve our own state of mind.

MOOD SPIRALS

If we find ourselves saying, "I can't do this!" or "I'm a failure as a parent," we need to realize that it is just our low mood talking. We cannot trust our thinking in low moods. At that moment we probably can't do very well, but we also need to realize that such a statement reflects only a passing thought at that moment—if we let it pass. If we get scared that we said it, and start dwelling on it, and believe it has implications beyond our mood at the moment—that it speaks to the very heart of our ability as a parent and means we never should have had children in the first place—then we will start to believe it. We will start to live it, and then we make it true. Yet, it's only a thought that popped into our heads! **When a thought pops in we have two choices: we can either let it pass through and not take it seriously, or we can dwell on it and make it real. We decide.**

To bring this back where we started, our key as parents is to find a nicer feeling for ourselves, which in turn means a nicer feeling for our family to live in. This feeling is the emotional climate our children live in, and it changes moment to moment with our moods. If we take the moments when we're feeling good to be with our child in a warm, relaxed lighthearted, caring way, to be with them and create a good feeling around them, we'll generally do pretty well as parents. Then, when we're in a low mood, if we become aware of our feelings and not take our thinking at that time so seriously, and simply let it pass and go into damage control if needed, the good moments will accumulate, and the overall emotional climate will become better and better. In other words, in a healthy emotional climate through a secure, responsive state, problems have a far better chance of being solved well.

MOODS IN ACTION

In my book, *Modello*, about how this Health Realization approach changed lives in two low-income, inner-city housing projects, I described a situation where moods came into play concerning a parent I called Carrie Mae. Carrie Mae was a nice woman who loved her children. She also had a violent temper. When her temper got riled up she was known to "go off" on anyone, anywhere, particularly on her own kids, and particularly when something bad would happen in school. At those times she was known to take her belt, storm over to the school, and "wail away" on her kid even in front of the principal.

One day, the principal phoned. Her son (in sixth grade) had just pulled a knife on another kid in school. Carrie Mae became livid. She grabbed her belt and stormed over to school.

But she had been learning about moods and how they affected interactions.

Halfway to the school, something popped into her head: "Wait a minute, I'm in a really bad mood right now. I'd better watch it."

When she arrived at the school, she simply picked up her son, brought him home, put him in his room, went to a friend's house, and stayed there for three hours. She stayed until she found that loving, caring feeling for her son come back.

She then went back to him and in a calm, caring tone said something like, "Honey, can you tell me what was going on with you, pulling a knife and all? Has something been going over at school?"

Shocked that he wasn't being beaten, her son said, "Yeah, these boys have been picking on me and I was really scared and I didn't know what to do."

Carrie Mae had no idea that this was going on. She had never taken the time to listen. They both cried and had a tremendous breakthrough in their relationship, and it lasted.

This is the power of understanding moods.

TAKING RESPONSIBILITY FOR WHAT HAPPENS IN OUR MOODS

Given the vast improvements in our own relationship with Jaime we now know that the only time we fall out of our wonderful feelings for each other is when we're in low moods. We all have our moments of low moods, but we know enough now to ride them out and not take personally what anyone says when in them. We know that our low mood thinking is not real—unless we make it be. What's real is the inner health and well-being and common sense that gets brought out through love and understanding.

When we're feeling low we know there is a good chance that our thinking is off, that our thoughts are feeding us faulty information. We understand that when in low moods we can't trust our thinking. We know that we can't take too seriously what our partners or children say to us at those times because it is only their low-mood-thinking talking. We sure wouldn't want our loved ones to take too seriously some of the things we have said and done in our low moods, so we can't be too overzealous at those times in taking what they throw at us too personally. Sure, we have bad thoughts at those times, but such thinking will look completely different later when our mood rises, so we would do well not to act on those thoughts.

To take responsibility for our own mood levels and how it affects our thinking and our subsequent actions is one of the most productive, most practical things we can do as parents.

KIDS UNDERSTAND MOODS

With Katie's husband away on business for a couple of weeks, she was left to take care of her two kids. Both kids were involved in dance classes, gymnastics and other sports, and Katie had to do all the transporting, organizing and running around by herself. She was beat and grumpy.

At the dinner table that night the kids were in great moods. Katie was not! All evening long she barked out orders, ordering them to do this and that, with no kindness or caring in her voice.

"Take your vitamins!" she barked.

"Mom."

"What?"

"Go to bed."

Her mother paused for a moment, stunned, then as if on automatic pilot, she nodded, "Okay," and made a beeline for the bedroom.

Intuitively, she knew that her kids knew more than she did at that moment.

* * *

A friend's child was having so much fun in day care that she did not want to leave when her mother came to pick her up. The mother, who was rushed and in a low mood, wanted her child to come along—now!

The child said, "I'm not going!"

"Yes you are."

"Nope," she said, shaking her head.

"Yes you are. Come along right now!"

"You're not my mommy!"

"What? Well, maybe you're not my daughter,"

"You can't say that!"

"Why not?"

"Because I'm going to like you later."

V. WHAT PROBLEM BEHAVIOR IS

My (then) seventeen year old son, my wife, and I took a trip to visit colleges. David was in a foul mood and taking it out on us. We knew it was only a profoundly low mood, but it was wearing on our nerves.

I was driving and, to him, I could do nothing right. He would criticize me and yap at me for practically every move I made.

"Would you like to drive, Dave?"

"No."

"Well, if you're not willing to drive, don't criticize my driving then."

I tried to keep my spirits high and make light of it, but finally he said something enormously rude and nasty, and it really got to me. In other words, I lost myself.

I told him I didn't appreciate what he said, and I didn't think I deserved it. Unfortunately, I let it put me into a low mood. It gripped me and I couldn't seem to let it go. So I separated myself from him to clear my head. We stopped to eat, and I decided that either he was going to have to change, or I wanted out. They could put me on a bus, and I'd go back home. I thought about it over lunch and told Judy that's what I wanted to do.

During lunch David decided to stay in the car to take a nap instead of eating. We got back in the car with Judy driving. I hadn't had a chance to say anything to Dave yet because he was just waking up. Then, because we couldn't seem to find our way back onto the highway, David started making rude comments to Judy.

She said, "That's it! I'm out of here!" and started driving toward the freeway to head home. "If you want to get out and stay, get out!"

Dave said, "Okay, let me out. I'll stay here myself."

Judy called his bluff. She pulled over and said, "Okay, get out!"

Dave didn't move.

By this time I had calmed down myself and said, "David, do you see what you're doing to people? I had just asked mom to put me on a bus and that I'd go because I didn't want to take this stuff from you anymore and, apparently, mom isn't going to take it any more either."

He said something to the effect that we were both stupid drivers.

I said, "But you said you weren't willing to drive! We don't know where we're going. We've never been here before. We're trying to find our way around. It's not so easy in a strange place. The idea is not to sit back and judge and criticize, but to enter into a partnership with us, so together we can figure out where we're going and how to do it best. That's how people help each other out."

I saw him soften a bit.

I continued. "Look, mom's about to leave here, and that will be all for this trip, so if that's what you really want, we can do that, but maybe, instead, would you be willing to commit yourself to treat us with respect for at least the rest of this trip?"

He uttered a faint, "Yes."

I turned to Judy. "Do you accept that?"

She said, "Yes."

The rest of our trip went great! Dave slipped a few times, but we reminded him about his commitment and that seemed to calm him down.

Later, he confided in us how scared he was about visiting colleges, and the prospect of being far away from home. He was taking it out on the place he felt safest—us! This was his tendency. Whenever he felt insecure about anything, he took it out on us.

BAD APPLES?

What is bad behavior?

Bad behavior is nothing more than people acting out of insecurity.

When people lack understanding they tend to be more insecure. When people are in low moods, they tend to be more insecure. When people have organic problems that irritate behavior centers in the brain, they tend to get frightened and act out (these people may also lack more controls). David happened to have all three going on inside him, and he was frightened. Since showing fear is not cool (after all, he was a teenager), he acted out.

It is extremely important for parents to realize that everything we call "bad behavior," "troublesome behavior," "troubled behavior" boils down to people acting out of insecurity.

This has enormous implications. By acting in troublesome or troubling ways, no child is trying to nail us, or to do something bad to us. They are only acting out of insecurity. They're frightened for some reason, and at that time don't know any other way to be. The way they act at those times is the only thing that makes sense to them, and they may not have a clue why they're doing it. In other words, it's the best they know how to do at that time.

INSECURITY AND INNOCENCE

Again, every child is always doing the best they know how at the time, given the way s/he sees things. Children are acting out of innocence.

So are we! We parents are only doing the best we know how at the time. We are innocent too.

Children are born without insecurity. It is something they have to learn. Usually, they learn it from us. Then they learn it from their close relatives, then from peers and school. No one tries to teach insecurity; that is the last thing we want. Yet, in our innocence, we do things that contribute to it.

As stated earlier, children are born into a world filled with wonder. Everything is new. There are so many new things to see, so many new smells, so many sounds, tastes, and a whole world to touch! It's the greatest amusement park imaginable. If babies start to feel physically uncomfortable they begin to cry. It's natural. Whatever it is—a hurting tummy, a yucky diaper—doesn't feel good, and crying is a natural response. The baby also soon learns that a cry will usually send a parent to the rescue, and that feels nice.

Tiny newborns begin to cry and we comfort them and we give them understanding, and we keep doing that until one day our child is crying for a really long time, and we get irritated (because we're in a low mood or we're frightened because we don't know what to do), and we may yap at the baby in a louder voice with an edge, and it scares her. Then she cries louder, and the cycle begins. The baby thinks to herself, "Woah, what's this!? I think I'd better watch out here. All is not as it seems." Or maybe the parent stops coming around when she's crying. What used to work doesn't any more.

Except when babies learn insecurity quite early in abusive or neglectful homes, in most homes they probably don't learn much insecurity until they begin to move around. Then they learn to crawl. Now they can get places, and suddenly their world vastly expands. They can get into things. "Yes!" they shout with glee.

When the crawler or toddler grabs certain items, the parents stop him and scold him, or sometimes slap him. The world has changed, and he doesn't understand it so well anymore. It's confusing. It can be scary. Insecurity begins to creep in.

Then when the child begins to walk, at first everyone is so thrilled–but the world vastly expands again, opening up a new world of possible things to get in to, and the cycle escalates.

Then the child begins to talk, and everyone is so excited. Then one day he apparently opens his mouth at the wrong time or the wrong thing comes out, and suddenly it seems that, at times, talking is no good, and everything becomes so confusing. Insecurity abounds.

Much insecurity, then, seems to occur simply by what we learn as we grow. There is almost no way that we parents can avoid having our children develop some insecurities. **The more we can help them feel secure, however, despite the difficulties they get into, the better off they are. Thus, the better off we are.**

When children feel insecure or fearful they act in strange ways—just as we do. Children act in any way they think will make the fear and insecurity go away, only they are not aware that they are thinking it. The only trouble is, the insecurity usually does not go away. In fact, the way kids act when they are insecure usually makes things worse—the same as when we act out of insecurity or fear.

Our children are innocent—just as we are. They don't know any better. If they did they would act differently. If they knew how to act in a way that would really make it better—instead of just thinking it will (but really producing the opposite)–they would. No one wants that kind of pain. Nobody likes the pain it causes, but they don't know how to do it any differently.

INSECURITY AS THOUGHT

It all comes down to the fact that they don't think they can do any differently or any better. The seed is thought. What's behind insecurity is thought. At the root lies thought. Thought can change.

When kids are acting out, the key for parents is to look at the way we think about our children at those times. We can either see the kid as purposely giving us a hard time, or we can see him as insecure, just acting out his insecurity without knowing any other way at the time.

Suppose we see the kid as giving us a hard time. How would we react?

Now suppose we see the kid as insecure and trying in any way he can to compensate for it. Would we react any differently?

From such different vantage points we would automatically treat the kid differently. What would be our natural inclination if we thought our kid was out to get us or purposely trying to do wrong, compared with our natural inclination if we thought our child was hurting inside and afraid?

If an infant has a crying fit, and his little arms flail away, and he hits us in the eye—and it really hurts—we don't hold it against the baby.

If a toddler, in a crying fit, little legs kicking away, kicks us in the shins, and it really hurts, would we hold it against him?

If a teenager, in a fit of rage, hormones kicking away, puts his fist through the wall, do we hold it against him?

Yet it's all insecurity.

If we see bad behavior as willful, we tend to want to control and punish. If we see bad behavior as acting out of insecurity, we ask ourselves how we can help take away his or her insecure thoughts.

MANIFESTATIONS OF INSECURITY

When people feel insecure they tend to see life in a narrow way, in a limited way, in a consistent way—given their particular style or their own personal way of reacting. Some kids have angry and violent responses. Some kids get sad and depressed. Some kids cheat and steal. Some kids yell and scream. Some kids get judgmental and put down their parents for the way they drive. Some kids take drugs and drink to excess. Some kids pick on others and do them harm. Some kids become sex abusers. Some kids grow up to physically or emotionally abuse their own kids or their spouses. The reason? They are all acting out of insecurity in their own ways. It is not that they are trying to be that way; they do not understand anything else.

How can we help them understand at a deeper level what is going on and help make them feel more secure?

WHAT TO DO

The first thing is not to take personally what they are doing. If they are acting out of insecurity, why would we take it personally? If we don't take it personally we don't need to react at that level. If we see their distress we will automatically feel compassion. If we take it personally, we will automatically be bothered.

Secondly, we can take a look at how we may be unknowingly passing on insecurity to our children. When the child exhibits inappropriate behavior the child is not at fault, their thoughts are. Thoughts lead to the feelings that lead to the behaviors that lead us to thoughts that make us react. Dr. Roger Mills gives an example: If a parent harbors a strong belief that his children cannot be happy unless they are more athletic, artistic, or educated, the parent unknowingly passes those beliefs onto the child in an overly concerned, anxious way which leads to insecurity. This child begins to think that his own well-being is contingent upon how well he does with respect to those "important" things. Then we get on him for not doing well. Yet, people do not respond well to threats. Threats are external motivation and they're scary. People do not do well when they're "running scared."

For instance, if I can't let go of the thought that my child needs a good grade I feel the tension and disappointment when she gets a poor grade. Instead, I could observe my feelings and know that it means I'm off track. I have other alternatives. I could encourage her and let her know I really care. If she doesn't make it, I know I tried. Besides, she's good at other things. Everyone is good at something. Maybe it means she will develop her other talents.

SUMMARY

When people are frightened and insecure they don't learn and grow well. What a child comes to think and feel about herself largely comes from us and the feeling we have about life, and what is acceptable to us and what is not. If our children are raised with warm, hopeful, radiant feelings, a warm, hopeful, radiant child is likely to emerge. We want to raise our children with a minimum of insecurity.

In summary, then, what does this suggest that we do as parents?

First, we want to look at ourselves to be sure we are raising our kids in a way that passes on to them as few of our insecurities as possible.

Then, if confronted with a problem behavior, we want to see it as insecurity instead of as a personal attack or affront; that they're lost and can't see any better way at the time.

Seeing the behavior as insecurity will make us naturally respond in a more helpful way than seeing it as a willful, malicious act. Seeing it as insecurity makes us somehow want to help relieve that insecurity and help them see a better way.

Does this mean that we let them get away with everything? Absolutely not! It simply means that if we see the child and the behavior differently we will naturally act differently.

The next chapter will help us see what to do.

VI. DISENGAGEMENT ~ TAPPING INTO COMMON SENSE TO GUIDE INTERACTIONS

Some years ago a huge truck jammed itself under a bridge on Storrow Drive in Boston and became stuck. Traffic backed up for miles. No one knew what to do. They called in engineers.

Stuck in traffic, an eight year old in one of the nearby cars said to his father, "Dad, why don't they just let some of the air out of the tires."

Out of the mouth of babes.

Our children have this capacity inside them if their minds are clear enough to hear it.

* * *

I am running barefoot on a beach scattered with many rocks. I keep my eyes fixed on the sand five feet ahead of me. I do not look where I put my feet. I step on no rocks.

What is going on? My feet seem to shift themselves as I move along. My natural intelligence is guiding me.

If I get distracted I step on a rock and hurt my foot.

* * *

Our son, David, was recruited to play basketball at a college in Massachusetts. Before he arrived the coach who recruited David left. A new coach came in. As a freshman David sat on the bench the entire season because the new coach played only seniors. As a sophomore he was forced into a starting role. As I watched him play I'm thinking,

"Gee, he's so much better than this. He's not taking any chances out there. Why isn't he playing up to his capability?"

I learned that the coach was screaming at the players to try to get them to play right. It was working against him. David was playing to not make a mistake so he wouldn't be screamed at and benched, instead of playing from his heart and just letting the game flow.

I asked Dave if he thought he was playing to avoid mistakes now instead of getting into the flow of his own game. He said yes. I asked him what he was thinking when he was scoring seemingly at will. He said, "Nothing."

I said, "Well, wouldn't it make sense to drop the thinking? You know what you're capable of doing when you're not thinking, just getting into the flow. The other kind of thinking is just a distraction and takes you away from your game."

My telling him this meant nothing. He had to feel it for himself. By the middle of the season the team was continually losing, and the coach was increasingly on their cases. Then one of the best players got kicked off the team for doing something stupid, the center became very ill when his mother died so he was out of action, and the point guard decided to transfer.

I said, "Well Dave, figure it this way, the coach can't possibly expect you guys to win now, so you've got nothing to lose. You may as well just go out there and have a good time playing your game."

The next game David scored over twenty points, and the next, and the next. The only difference was that his head cleared. The team even won a couple of games because everyone was playing so loosely. Then, thinking they had a chance to win again, the coach once again started getting on their backs. Low and behold, the team started losing. But for the rest of the season David never looked back. He had gained confidence in his own ability. He knew he could do it now, no matter what his coach did. Because his head had cleared he had clicked into a higher level of functioning, which made him tap into the purity of his skills and focus, unencumbered by any extraneous thoughts such as how well he was doing.

Acting out of a clear head made David play at his peak. His wisdom took over. This is what happens to everyone when they operate out of a clear head, when extraneous thoughts subside. This is what happens to us as parents.

THE CAPACITY FOR CLARITY AND INSIGHT

Unencumbered by extraneous thoughts we all have this capacity to be at our peak, to act out of our peak. It is built into us.

To have it, all we have to do to is ask ourselves where we are or what we are doing when we get our best ideas.

In every case it is when our mind is relaxed. Whether we are in the shower or doing dishes or waking from sleep or taking a walk or knitting or driving a car or meditating or on vacation or whatever, our minds are relaxed.

When the mind is relaxed insights pop into our heads from a deeper intelligence. This wisdom often takes the form of common sense. We often say to ourselves, "Of course! Why didn't I see that before? It is so obvious."

The reason we didn't see it before is because our minds were filled up, scrambling, processing too much information, pushing our insecurity buttons. We are often too close to something to see the big picture. But if we step back and clear our heads, it appears.

When we are filling our heads with information, processing data and running programs like a computer, we do not have room to pick up fresh, new, clear ideas, as a radio receiver will—if the channel is clear. A head full of grinding away and processing will not allow our wisdom and common sense to flow in and speak to us.

DISENGAGEMENT EQUALS THE ABILITY TO STEP BACK AND SEE

Jasmine, a two-year-old, was driving her mother, Betsy, crazy. Every morning when Betsy needed Jasmine to get ready to leave the house to get to an appointment on time, Jasmine would stall. When her mother went to make her get ready, Jasmine would throw a temper tantrum. Her mother would say to her, "If you don't come right now, I'm going to leave without you." Jasmine would get scared and cry as her mother grabbed her to get ready.

Betsy, a single mother, is too riled up and frustrated to see her way out of this cycle. Every morning she anticipates the worst and gets it. Every morning she does the most expedient thing at the time. Yet, if she were to take a step back, she would see a few things. Betsy would see that Jasmine is learning some lessons, only not the lessons Betsy wants her to learn.

What lessons is Jasmine learning? First, Jasmine is learning that if someone scares you enough, you cooperate; otherwise, why bother? You may as well stall until you get scared enough.

Jasmine has not learned the second lesson yet, but it is only a matter of time. Soon she will learn that her mother is not really serious about leaving her behind, that it is just an idle threat not to be taken seriously. So Jasmine doesn't really need to listen after all. Further, by lying to her, Jasmine will also learn that it is okay to lie; that what's okay for her mother is okay for her.

Jasmine is also learning that power and force ultimately prevail. She is engaging in a battle of wills. Both are immersed in a power struggle. Her mother wins eventually because she is more powerful. But it is only a matter of time—maybe ten or thirteen more years—before the tables are turned.

Seeing this comes from taking the time to step back and ask, "What is my child learning from what I'm saying or doing?" Then, common sense steps in and asks, "Okay, what do I want my child to learn instead?"

Disengaged from the struggle, answers come to mind. "I'd rather not have my child learn fear from me. I'd rather have her learn that she's safe with me." It would be best, then, not to try to coerce her with fear. Stepping back even further, Betsy would have realized that because the State took Jasmine away from her for a few months, and shunted her around from one foster home to another, Jasmine is scared to death of being left behind again, and by saying, "I'll leave you if you don't come now!" is only exacerbating her fears.

"I'd like my child to be able to count on me and what I say." It would be best, then, to follow through with what is said. "If I say I'm going to leave her behind, I have to be willing to do it. Am I willing to? No!" It would be best, then, to find something to say that isn't a lie.

"I'd rather not have my child learn that the only time she has to obey is when she's forced. I don't want her to learn that life is about power struggles. I'd rather have her learn that life is about cooperation and helping each other out. I'd like to have her learn that when a commitment is made, you keep it, whether you feel like it at the time or not." It would be best, then, to disengage from the power struggle, and show her caring and firmness at the same time.

With this new perspective, we might say, "Honey, I really don't like having to do this to you. I know you don't like it, and I'm sorry. But mommy has an appointment that she's got to go to, and I can't leave you behind. So you have to come with me now, sweetie."

Due to past history, of course, Jasmine will throw a temper tantrum and scream that she's not going. She's used to it, and it gets attention.

"Sweetie, it's not a question of whether you will go. It's how you will go. It's so much nicer for everyone if you come nicely. It's nicer for you too. You tell me how you would like to do it. What can I do to help you?"

If she still kicks and screams and moans, we would want to make it a non-issue. As much as humanly possible, we would want to not respond. As gently as humanly possible under the circumstances, and saying as little as possible, we would simply do what we had to do to get her ready, and not buy in to her temporary insanity. This would show her that there is no issue; she is just going to come with us.

We might be tempted to say, "We'll do something nice together later when we get back," but we have to be careful. First, we must be absolutely certain that if we say it we will do it, because we want her to be able to count on us. Second, we don't want her to think that she'll agree to go only to get some reward later. On the other hand, we want to do something nice with her later—on general principle. So it depends how it feels at the time.

By stepping back and gaining new perspective, we can see what we really want to accomplish in the long run. Then we only have to do what makes sense, because it is only common sense. With a clear mind, our common sense appears.

CLEARING THE HEAD

When we feel the need to discipline a child the best thing that can happen is for our common sense to interact with their common sense.

This will happen best when both sets of minds are clear.

When we are relaxed, clear, calm, and have nothing on our minds, the human mind naturally functions in a healthy way. Having concerns on our minds takes us away from healthy functioning. If what our child is doing is causing us concern, we could take it in stride and not let it get us down because it will lower our spirits. When our spirits are low, we do not think well, because we do not have access to our wisdom and common sense.

Backing off, taking a breather and regaining our bearings sets us up to be more in touch with what our wisdom tells us about what to do. It also helps our children to be more relaxed so they can be more in touch with their common sense.

TIME OUT?

One way that parents can help children calm down and clear their heads is by having them take "time out"; meaning, separate the child from the situation *until* they regain their bearings. Many parents, however, use time out as a punishment, relegating the child to a chair or bed for sometimes a half-hour or more. They say, "If you don't do what I say, you'll go to time out!"

While this is certainly better than smacking a kid, it is really an inappropriate use of time out. Time out should be for only as long as it takes a child to calm down and regain her bearings. When she has calmed down and can deal with people reasonably again, she can return because she will have her wits about her. Saying something like, "You'll have to take some time out for yourself until you calm down, then we'd love you to come back when you're ready," would be a very appropriate statement.

WISDOM AND COMMON SENSE

Every parent has the common sense and wisdom to be a good parent. It is built into us.

When parents can see their children's ability to access their innate, common sense, and treat them supportively and appropriately instead of negatively and punitively they will see this common sense emerge. When children are able to access their own natural feelings of self-respect, respect for others, and unconditional self-esteem they will naturally function in a responsible way—simply by using their own innate capacity for common sense.

We do not have to build this capacity in a child! **Children are naturally inclined toward feelings of self-esteem, positive motivation, and respect. They have a natural capacity to understand natural consequences of their behavior.**

This capacity exists prior to children learning any beliefs about what they need. If these natural tendencies are allowed to develop in our children without unnecessary interference, anxiety, or pressure, they will develop to their full potential whatever unique talents and abilities they possess. In other words, without the accumulated beliefs and attitudes that lead them to think, for example, that they must have approval or acceptance, they would naturally have access to their well-being and their wisdom and common sense. Only when children have been programmed with insecure, self conscious thoughts, do they make the wrong decisions—unless they simply do not understand something [more on this in Chapter VIII].

FAITH AND TRUST

Every parent has a deeper consciousness, a deeper intelligence, built-in common sense to allow us to know what is best to do in any given situation with our children. We're often just too caught up to see it. Or, we doubt that we have this capacity–we don't trust that we have it.

Being caught up and not trusting it are the only things that get in our way. We could have the same faith that our child's innate health and wisdom is there as we do that the sun is behind the clouds even in a blizzard. No one has to convince us. All we have to do is watch closely, and we will see it emerge from time to time.

FROM A DISTANCE

The reason that Carrie Mae (the woman who stormed over to the school with belt in hand in Chapter IV) knew how to approach her son after she calmed down was not because she had learned particular parenting techniques; rather, it was because from a clear head she knew what to do.

This is called disengaging, backing off, observing the situation from a distance with a calm state of mind. When we do this, we will usually know what to do. And even if we don't, our attitudes will be right, so we won't go too far wrong.

If we make the wrong decision because our heads were not as clear as we thought they were, we can always regroup, apologize that we blew it, and get back on the right track.

Our children get caught up just as we do. Wherever we can, the more we can give them some breathing space to step back and evaluate what they might do differently, the better off they (and we) will be.

When we pressure children, yell at them, tell them we don't trust them, take over for them, we do not give them a chance to engage their common sense. They are too busy scrambling and running for cover.

HEALTHY MENTAL FUNCTIONING

To summarize this in another way, inside everyone is a state of healthy psychological functioning. Everyone experiences it from time to time. Hardly a day goes by that we don't experience it for at least a moment, but it is so natural we don't notice. We don't notice that our insights come from the quiet.

The first step is to know it's there and trust it.

Secondly, we need to learn to disengage, back off, and observe from a distance. If we feel ourselves having negative feelings, we have to get ourselves back on track before we can teach our children anything.

When we approach a situation with an unencumbered mind, from a quiet place, with a clear head, we will naturally draw out our children's wisdom and common sense.

Suppose we come home from work tired, and our child wants to play. She keeps at us because she wants attention from not being around us all day. Here we have two choices: We could spend time with the child right then, or we could say, "Ohhh, honey, I want to play with you, but I'm really tired right now, and if you just give me some time to myself to take a break for maybe ten or twenty minutes (depending on the child's age), then we'll do something special together." Which would be better?

In the first approach we would likely be with the child begrudgingly, and she would feel it. In the second, we

would be much more present—because we took the time to back off. If it is a very young child, we might have to stay in the room while we take a rest. If the child keeps bugging us we may have to show them where the hands on the clock will have to be and tell them the hands will move faster if they play by themselves for a while and forget about the clock—and then don't react.

Children don't want to be in conflict any more than we do.

If we dropped out of the conflict—if we detached from it—and then observed the conflict from a distance, we would know better how to resolve that conflict. We would then be better able to approach the child again with a feeling of love and with access to our wisdom.

Once the emotions of the moment die down a bit and people take a step back from the situation they have more access to their wisdom and common sense; then they can see things in a different light. Then, together, in a nonthreatening atmosphere, they are better equipped to work on solutions.

RAPPORT

Once we disengage and have access to our wisdom, it would be nice if our wisdom could be communicated. The pathway for this communication is through rapport.

Rapport is little more than what we talked about in Chapter I. It means a feeling of closeness. Rapport is the extent to which we feel understanding for our child. Rapport is the path to drawing out the best in our children.

The more rapport we feel, the more our children will come to us with their concerns. The more rapport we feel, the more they will confide in us.

If they feel guilt-tripped by us, we lose rapport. If they feel put down, we lose rapport. If they are afraid of our reaction, we lose rapport. If they're afraid that we won't understand and will just come down hard on them, we lose rapport.

Little children are always coming to us to tell us things. This is their natural state. This is what they want to be able to continue to do, even as they get older. They want to be able to discuss things with us. They only lose the desire when we lose rapport.

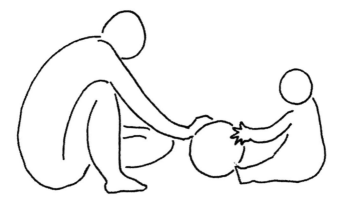

The degree of closeness that we have is the potential that we have for influencing our children in a positive way. If we have rapport, our children will listen to us better. They will think better around us. Our relationship with our children is like a savings account. When we feel closer we put in deposits. When we feel distant we make withdrawals. In a secure, responsive state we naturally make deposits. In insecure, reactive states we make withdrawals—unless we are aware that we are about to make a withdrawal if we act on what we're thinking or open our big mouths.

Dr. George Pransky says that the secret to rapport is being committed to "happy endings." This does not mean letting children have their way. It does not mean getting our way. It means that we both need to be satisfied with the result. It means that, within the right feeling, we are committed to working it through to resolution, no matter how long it takes, and feeling okay about what happens. We may not be able to agree on everything; that's understandable. On some issues we might have to agree to disagree if we can't get anywhere. However, if we truly commit ourselves to satisfaction and a feeling of resolve on both sides, and hang in until it happens, we will achieve it.

When both we and our children walk away from nearly every interaction feeling okay, rapport stays high.

Rapport is the foundation for listening (Chapter VII). It is the pathway to teaching (Chapter VIII) and discipline (Chapter IX).

VII. DEEP LISTENING[*]

A child in Judy's day care center and one of her staff suddenly were not getting along. At the end of the day Judy needed to have an important discussion with them. She asked our daughter to help out during the discussion by watching the child's younger brother. Jaime willingly agreed.

Jaime then received a phone call from a friend inviting her to dinner. She wanted to go. Judy said her discussion would last for about ten minutes.

Ten minutes passed. Jaime came downstairs to see if she could go, but Judy was still engaged in heavy conversation. Judy said they needed more time. Jaime went back upstairs. She came down again after another five minutes to an even heavier conversation.

Judy said, "Jaime, it's going to take me another minute. Then I'll drive you over there when I'm finished."

Getting irritated, Jaime said, "Well, can I walk then?"

Judy said, "You can walk if you want, but it's going to take me another minute."

After the heavy conversation ended Judy came back upstairs to find Jaime gone. The child had been left alone.

Later, when Jaime came back in from her dinner, Judy landed on her: "How could you have left the child alone? I asked you to do me a favor and you agreed. That's irresponsible!"

---

[*] Note to reader: For next three chapters especially, it is far more important to absorb an overall sense of this approach, rather than get lost in the details. What is presented is not a series of techniques, it is more of a stance or a general direction.

67

Jaime said, "What do you mean? You asked me to watch the kid for ten minutes, and I did. You told me I could walk, so I did."

"The kid could have gotten hurt left alone. I told you I'd be another minute."

"But you told me I could walk. I didn't know it was so important about this kid."

"That's not true, Jaime! I told you!"

Heads butted. Both became increasingly frustrated.

I am almost embarrassed to say that, again, I was listening to all this and, again, because I was not the one caught up in the emotions of the moment I heard something.

I said, "Hold on a moment. I think the two of you had two different perceptions of the situation. Then you each acted based on your different perceptions."

Jaime said she thought that was right, but she was still riled up.

In my kindest voice I said, "Jaime, do you see any grain of truth to what your mother is saying?"

"Yes."

"What is it?"

"That I shouldn't have run out on this kid without making sure it was okay, because he could have gotten hurt."

I turned to Judy. "Do you see a grain of truth in what Jaime is saying?"

"Yes, that when I said she could walk, she thought that meant she was free to go."

There is always a grain of truth in the other side. But how would we ever know unless we truly listened to that other side?

The other person's side makes perfect sense to her or him. Both sides are logical, given the way each person sees it. In the instance above neither could see it, not only because they were too caught up to see the other's logic but also because they were not truly listening to each other. They were too busy defending their own positions. We all tend to defend our own positions. We do this instead of listening. We do it far more than we realize.

KNOWING HOW TO RESPOND

In the previous chapter we learned to disengage so our minds could clear to allow access to our wisdom. We also learned to be sure our rapport is right. Does this mean we are now ready to take action? No! **Before we act or say anything we have one more task: to listen!** This step is essential. Yet, of all parenting tasks, listening to children is probably the one we are worst at, this author/parent included.

First, by truly listening with undivided attention children can feel that we care about them and take them seriously. This is not news.

The real purpose of listening to our children in any situation is so we know how to best respond to them.

Read that again.

How would we know the best thing to do, how would we know what to teach them, if we did not understand everything we needed to know about a situation?

Suppose when our children do something wrong our first, usual response is to yell. When we yell, they run for cover to protect themselves. If our first, usual response is to nag, they become oblivious. Suppose our first response is to listen. When we truly listen at a deep level, they become more attentive and responsive. Which would we rather have?

Since most of us are not used to doing it, listening at a deep level may take an adjustment.

LISTENING FOR WHAT?

We want to listen for what we really need to hear. Ironically, what we really need to hear has little or nothing to do with their words, with the content of what they are saying. In fact, paying too much attention to their words may keep us from hearing what we really need to hear. Essentially, we want to listen for three things:

1. for the meaning behind the words;

2. for how the child makes sense of her or his world and, if necessary, for the grain of truth in what s/he is saying;

3. for what specific thoughts (that the child doesn't see or understand) are keeping the child stuck or upset.

Let's explore each of these in detail.

1. First, we want to hear the meaning behind the words.

One way to grasp this is, if children were unable to use words, what would they be trying to say to us? Can we hear the real message? If anyone is wondering how we could possibly hear a message without words, interestingly this is a skill we already have. We naturally use this skill with infants. It does not take long to learn that different types of cries mean completely different things. This is listening beyond words, for there are no words to fall back on. Unfortunately, soon after children learn to speak our language, we tend to leave this skill behind. Children always use two languages at once: their words, and what they are really trying to say. What they are trying to say is far more important.

When my daughter, Jaime, said to me, "You don't understand kids!" [Chapter I], those were her words, but she was really trying to say: "If you want me to respond well, you have to show me love first. You have to say it with love."

Why didn't she just come out and say it then?

She did not know how. If she knew how to say it, she would have.

To be able to relate to this better, try sometime to describe "being in love" to someone who has never been in love before. What would you say to them? You've got the words, right? It is not so easy. Or try to describe the color "red" to someone who is color-blind? Or try to describe a spiritual experience to someone, using words. Or, even harder, try to describe the game of baseball to someone from another country who never saw a baseball game before. Sometimes words are simply inadequate. We know a lot more than we can actually express. So it is with kids. We cannot just listen to the words because we will miss a whole lot.

If we assume that our children do not have the words to express what they would like to really express to us, we would have to pay a lot more attention. We would have to find out more. We would have to ask them questions before telling them anything; something like—

"Tell me more about that." or,

"Can you give me an example of what you mean?" or,

"Explain what you mean again so I can understand better."

When we ask such questions our ear is then tuned to what makes sense to them about what they are saying. **We could really learn something from what makes sense to them.** We could learn more about them. We could learn more about how they are seeing the situation at hand which is causing them to react as they did or to behave as they do or to feel as they do. If we truly listened to them we might even have an insight about something they said that never occurred to us before. If we are too busy being "right" or "the authority" or defending our positions, we will never hear it. This moves us to the second point.

2. Second, we want to listen for how the child makes sense of his or her world, and for the grain of truth in what s/he is saying.

Not only do we want to know what lies behind children's words, but we want to know the truth of it to them. We want to be able to see their truth as they see it.

The example beginning this chapter illustrates what is meant by a "grain of truth." Everyone sees each situation according to how they see the world. This is their truth. If we listen closely we can hear their truth as they see it.

Given that each child sees each situation in a unique way that makes perfect sense to her or him, our job as listener is to see it as they see it. We want to keep inquiring until we are struck by something like, "Oh, I see how she could have come to that conclusion," or, "Oh, I can relate to his logic here."

To hear the grain of truth we cannot carry any preconceptions because we will only be listening to ourselves.

LISTENING TO DRAW OUT UNDERSTANDING

Sometimes we can hear things that the other person does not even understand. This story is a case in point:

I sat next to a young woman on an airplane. We began talking. She was a very intelligent student who had jumped right from college to graduate school and had not yet been out in the "real world." After a while she began talking about a new book by Naomi Wolfe that presented an alternative view of feminism which made her furious. Innocently I asked if she had read the book.

She said, "No," then became silent. After a few moments she said, "I'll bet you think I'm pretty narrow-minded, to be saying those things without having read the book."

Not being a fool, I decided to keep my mouth shut.

Then she said, "Sometimes I think that if you're too open-minded the stuff you know leaks out of your head like a sieve, so it's not good to be too open-minded."

I looked at her, puzzled. Was she joking or serious? By the look on her face I could tell that she was trying to make light of it but, deep down, she was quite serious. That was pretty much the end of the conversation.

The next morning, as I was taking a morning run, something popped into my head that made me realize what she was talking about. Here was a young woman with a head full of ideas. For some reason those ideas defined her life, defined who she considered herself to be. For some reason she desperately needed the world to make sense to her, and when it was challenged she felt lost, she no longer knew who she was, so she desperately had to cling to what she knew. I don't know why, but I was absolutely certain of this.

Certainly that was a deeper level of listening than I had used when talking with her. At the time I couldn't hear it because I was too caught up in the content of what she was saying, and whether I agreed or disagreed. When my head cleared, when I wasn't even thinking about it, it occurred to me what her world was like.

I never saw her again, but if I had, I could have asked her questions that perhaps would have helped both of us to gain more perspective on her world. I could have asked her,

"What do you make of the fact that this woman's perspective upsets you so much?" I could have sought out her grain of truth. It would have been a fascinating conversation. All because of deep listening! But again, so long as I focused on how much I disagreed with her, I missed an opportunity to really learn something. I could have gained a deeper understanding.

A CLEAR MIND

There is only one way to listen for deeper understanding: We have to empty our minds, clear our heads, so our wisdom can listen instead of filtering it through our programmed beliefs [Chapter III].

If we truly want to know what our children do and do not understand about any given situation, our minds must be free from everything we think we know. This is often most difficult for parents to do. We carry in us what we think is right and wrong, and we tend to filter what we hear through those screens.

Some clarification is in order about what it means to listen with a clear mind. Of course, the mind is almost never completely empty because various thoughts keep popping into it. The question is, which of those thoughts are relevant and which are not. **Listening with a clear mind really means dismissing those thoughts that are not relevant to our understanding.**

For example, when my son was yapping at me for not driving as well as he thought he could, I first had the thought, "I can't believe he's getting on my case about driving when I'm trying to figure out where I'm going and he's not taking any responsibility for it!" My mistake was taking that thought seriously, taking it to heart, when I should have dismissed it as irrelevant to my understanding. Next I had the thought, "I'm being insulted. I'm offended!"

The downward thinking spiral had already begun. Instead of taking it and running with it, I should have dismissed that thought too. Had I dismissed it, my mind would have had room for another thought. With my wits about me I might have thought, "Gee, what he's doing doesn't really make sense; what is he really trying to say here?" I might have stepped back and reflected upon why he was doing this at this moment. "What is going on with him?" With a clearer head another thought may have popped in: "Well, he's going to be going off to college; maybe he's insecure about it and taking it out on me." Now, that thought sounds interesting! I would not want to dismiss that thought yet. I would want to put that one on the back burner of my mind and explore it a little more, perhaps ask him some questions about it. Then another thought might pop in: "Maybe he's in too low a mood right now to answer any questions." Another thought worth considering! Then I get another: "But damn it, he has no right to insult me! I can't let him get away with that!" That one sounds familiar, suspiciously like what happens when I'm running scared. I can dismiss that one.

The above is an example of dismissing thoughts that are irrelevant to help us keep our minds as clear as possible. All it takes is awareness of which thoughts aid understanding (ones that sound fresh and new) and which do not (ones that sound like old, familiar news). We want to dismiss the latter thoughts as irrelevant the same way we would naturally dismiss a thought during this conversation such as, "I wonder what I need to buy at the store today?"

One of the biggest blocks to deep listening is that we will get a thought about something the talker says, and our minds will follow that thinking and lose the talker. If we are aware of this, we will recognize it while it's happening, and that recognition will bring us back to the moment. We will be present with our children again.

LISTENING FOR UNDERSTANDING

In short, we want to listen for what we truly want to be listening for: understanding. We want to be in a state of puzzlement until what our child did or said makes sense to us from his/her perspective. We want to listen and dismiss thoughts until we have a deep grasp of the true message behind all the garbage, until we get to the very bottom of what our child is saying.

For example, if our child is lying about something, we want to listen and ask questions until we understand how it made sense to him to think that he had to lie, and what made him think lying would work. See, there's even a grain of truth—for him—in a lie. Lest anyone conclude from this that I am suggesting to go along with or agree with whatever the kid came up with—not so! Just because we understand does not mean we have to agree. Yet, understanding must come first; any agreement or disagreement can come later. Most often we agree or disagree first and never get to the understanding. In so doing we miss what we need to hear to guide us in what to do.

Let's go back to the example in Chapter I, when Judy and Jaime got into that "fight." The only difference in what I could hear and what Judy could hear was that she was too close to the situation, and I was detached. Had I been the one caught up she would have been the far better listener.

Let's examine what Judy heard. At first she heard, "Jaime doesn't care about me enough to clean up, knowing how tired I am when I come home from work." Later in the conversation she heard, "It's a power issue; I'm taking her power away from her." From my greater distance, my clearer mind at the time, I heard, "She's not feeling enough love from us." Same words, different listening, different understandings, different points from which to build communication and subsequent action.

If lecturing turns kids off, asking the right questions at the right time opens them up (and remember, moods tell us when the right time is). Further, the listener will then pick up on our respect–because we are truly trying to understand–and s/he will respond accordingly. **The tone will come out right if our hearts are in the right place. Our hearts will be in the right place if we sincerely want to understand.**

LISTENING TO SPAWN INSIGHT

At best, we want to engage in the type of listening that draws our children out of their own typical ways of thinking and enables them to have new insights. In other words, besides attempting to understand their worlds, if we see something that we don't think they understand, it would be worthwhile to ask questions that might help them see something new. It would be wonderful if they were to see something that they never saw before that draws them into a zone of deeper thinking or exploration.

By contrast, if what they hear from us puts them on the defensive or on the spot, unwittingly creating insecurity, children will retreat into the narrow, personal zone of defending themselves. To avoid this we could first assume that whatever the child is saying is true in her world, so we would first want to try to see it with as in-depth an understanding as we possibly can. As Dr. George Pransky says, **we have to make it our business to have a healthy respect for what is being said and, if we do not have this respect, assume that we have not heard it yet.** Then we can inquire until we reach the point where we can say, "Oh, I can relate to that. I can respect that, at least from his point of view We want to get touched by our child's view.

Instead of disagreeing or agreeing we want to find whether there is any merit in his idea that will aid our understanding.

The most common difficulty preventing us from hearing the understanding we need is that our own judgments or opinions. These interfere. They fill our heads and block out understanding. Then that becomes what our kids hear from us. By contrast, as deep listeners we want everything out of our minds except, "What is this person trying to get across to me?" We want to clear away all extraneous debris. We then feel closer because we'll be that much more connected.

By way of illustration, suppose our kid comes home saying, "I hate school."

The most unproductive listening is no listening at all–a response, such as, "No you don't. You always say you like school," or worse, "What did you do wrong now!?"

More productive listening might be to ask, "What do you mean, honey? What's troubling you about school?"

If the response is, "I just do!" or "It sucks" or "Nothing!" or "Never mind!" that's a signal that we have to inquire further (but now may not be the right time).

We may want to follow up with something like, "Did something bad happen to you at school?"

In the process of inquiring we may find out that other kids are picking on our child, or that a teacher or administrator is yelling at him for what he considers to be no good reason.

"Yeah, I can see how you could hate school at this moment."

The idea is to get him to the point where he might be open enough to explore further. Listening from the heart is what got us here.

During the listening that would go on in the exploration process we might ask our child further questions to inspire insights (but remember, it is impossible to make insights happen in another person). To get closer we might ask something like, "What do you think goes on in someone's mind to make them give other people a hard time?" or "What do you think might be going on with him for him to do that to you?" or "What does it mean to you that he does that?"

Our child may never have thought about things in this way before—he was too busy protecting himself—and the answer may hold possible insights. Or not! At this point it becomes an exploration, an inquiry to find the root of the issue, what lies behind what is on the surface.

We parents are often too quick to try to find solutions without thoroughly listening first.

It is also possible for us to get our own insights through the listening process. George Pransky provides another example: Suppose our children have just made a mess in the house. By questioning and deeply listening all of a sudden we might be struck with something like, "Wow, the reason they make a mess all the time is because of how carefree they are, how much they throw themselves so completely into the moment, and then they just move on to the next moment. Their vitality is really such a wonderful thing." That's an example of an insight, something we didn't see before. From that perspective we might want to take a different approach to cleaning up, such as building upon their vitality by making a game out of cleaning up, or going the opposite route and helping them see the value in slowing down from time to time to regain perspective and that stopping to clean helps people slow down.

LISTENING AS A GUIDE TO TEACHING

This brings us to the third message we want to listen for. This is particularly important if we want to use the situation as an opportunity to teach.

3. We want to listen for what thoughts (that s/he doesn't understand) are keeping the child stuck or upset?

Listening is the bridge between having a clear mind and knowing what we need to teach our children at the time. Unless we listen, we do not know exactly what our children really need to learn in any given situation. Listening should drive our actions.

Suppose we take our six-year-old shopping and the child sees a toy that she wants. We tell her, "I'm sorry, sweetie, you can't have that. It belongs to the store." Suddenly the child throws a temper tantrum. We feel all eyes upon us. We have all witnessed similar scenes and have seen a variety of parental reactions, such as yelling, smacking, yanking the kid bodily out of the store, putting up with the screaming with a pained expression on one's face. At this point most of us tend to listen to our own embarrassment. We only want the kid to shut up. We react accordingly.

If we were to set aside our own embarrassment, take a step back and truly listen, we might see that our own embarrassment isn't the most important issue; that what is going on is merely a symptom of larger issues.

We might hear that the problem is really that our child's state of mind is off. What does a child need when her state of mind is off? Love and understanding!

We might see the larger issue as, our child doesn't understand how to keep from getting out of control and how to keep her bearings when things aren't going her way.

This then becomes what we need to teach. Or, we might hear that before she went into the store the child's expectations were unrealistic. This may help us to make an adjustment. Whatever we hear helps us see what we need to teach.

QUESTIONS THAT AID LISTENING

In summary, here are examples of the types of questions that may help us to listen better.

The first type of question is not something we ask of the other person. It is what we ask of ourselves in preparation for listening. With questions like this, we "engineer" our minds to hear the answers:

* **I'd like to get touched by how he sees his world.**

* **I'd like to understand what makes sense to her about this.**

* **I'd like to see what he sees that I don't.**

* I'd like to understand what she is trying to get across to me.
* I'd like to understand what he is not seeing that would help him.
* I'd like to see what she doesn't realize.

Once our minds are engineered to listen for these answers, when engaged in actual conversation or when watching or observing, we actually want to forget about these questions. This may seem like a contradiction, but it isn't. To hear the answers, our heads must be clear; we want nothing on our minds. Then, thoughts will pop into our heads. Some of these thoughts will be answers to those questions. But we don't necessarily want to take the first answer that comes along. When a thought pops in, we want to dismiss it to keep our minds clear. We want to keep dismissing them until certain thoughts keep coming back, and we feel sure that we know what's going on.

During the conversation, to aid our understanding, we might ask questions such as these:
* **Can you help me understand this better?**
* **Tell me more. Can you say it in another way?**
* **Do you mean _____?**
* **What do you make of this?**

Questions such as these draw the talker into a zone of deeper thinking. Don't forget, we want to listen until we have a healthy respect for how our child sees things. Only our own judgments, opinions, and disagreements keep us from hearing what they see.

Suppose we had asked our twelve year old to clean the living room and came back to find papers and books and coats scattered everywhere. Our usual thought might be, "He didn't do what I told him!" We might attribute his actions to any number of motivations and land on him for whichever we believed true. To truly listen we might ask the child some questions. We might find that the child doesn't have the same idea about what "clean" is as we do, that the kid really did think he had cleaned up because he did sweep the floor. We didn't take into consideration that he doesn't have the same "eyes" for the situation as we have. Once we know this, instead of getting on his case our course of action is to help him understand, to learn about how to look at a room and tell whether it is clean, to connect with his own common sense about it.

Suppose we tell our fifteen year old that she can't go to a party, and she slams the door in frustration. Not listening well, we might get on her for slamming the door or remind her who is boss and what we say goes and we don't want to hear any complaints. If we were truly listening we may hear that our decision does not make sense to her, that she doesn't understand the situation as we understand it, that she can't see how we arrived at that decision, that she has no idea what all the factors were that we took into consideration. This might cause us to take pause and examine how we did arrive at this decision. Did we go through any process at all? In fact do we ourselves really understand exactly why we think that, in this case, it is not a good idea to go, and why? Before we check to see if it makes sense to her, we had better check to see if it makes sense to us, and search our own hearts for the reason we've decided this. Perhaps through this process we may even reach a different conclusion and see that, in this instance, she can go, because we don't have a good reason why not. Through our listening we might see that the reason she is rebelling is because we are not working out decisions like this as a team so that everyone has the same understanding.

Suppose we believe, instead, that our kids go out of their way to give us a hard time. If we really listened we would likely find this the case in only the rarest of instances. We would hear that it is almost never a matter of willfulness. Instead, we want to give our kids the benefit of the doubt, see their insecurity, see their state of distress, see their innocence, see what they don't understand. Truly listening will tell us and will guide us in the direction of what we need to teach.

[P.S. It might also be worthwhile to use the type of listening recommended in this chapter on your partner or spouse. ☺]

This book has been pointing to an understanding of life that at first may sound strange. In a nutshell, it is about how we function as human beings; how the interplay of three principles creates the experience we have of life, including the experience we have of our children. The three principles are: 1) *Mind* (the intelligence behind life, the life force, the formless energy that is the source of life itself); 2) *Thought* (the power to create); 3) *Consciousness* (the power to experience). We can only experience what our thoughts create.

Forget about the words! In essence, this means that while it looks like our experiences are coming to us from the world out there—for example, when our children act up it looks for all the world that we're upset because of what they did—really our experiences and feelings are coming from our own thinking. Our experience always comes to us from within, even though it appears otherwise. If we are upset or angry with what our children are doing it is only because we are seeing our kids and the situation in ways that are making us upset and angry. If we saw it differently we would experience it differently. And when a new, different thought comes along, our experience of that situation and of our kids will change.

This does not mean that we make up what happens to us. It does mean that, without realizing it, we make up how we experience what happens to us—and that changes with new thinking. We think our parenting problems are caused by our kids, when they are really caused by the way we are seeing our kids. When we see our children in a different light, new worlds of possibilities unfold before us.

For additional resource materials based upon this understanding, visit the Resource Center at www.pomhr.com, *or call the NorthEast Health Realization Institute at 802-563-2730. For additional information about this understanding, visit the Sydney Ranks Institute for Innate Health website at* www.sbiih.org, *or call the NorthEast Health Realization Institute at (802) 563-2730.*

VIII. TEACHING KIDS WHAT THEY NEED TO LEARN

What is the most important thing we can teach our children?

It may be for children to learn to tap into their own wisdom and common sense, so they know what makes the most sense in any given situation. This might be called "self-reliance."

The pathway to self-reliance is through the heart. When dealing with our children, just as we want to take a step back to engage our own wisdom and common sense, so we want our children to be able to take a step back and see the big picture so they can engage their common sense to know how best to proceed.

We can help our children gain self-reliance not by teaching them what we know or about our conclusions, but by teaching them what we take into account in reaching our conclusions.

PREPARATION FOR TEACHING

Again we need to remind ourselves continually that in trying to teach children anything, they will hear and react to the quality of our feeling, not our words. If they hear us being judgmental, they will only hear the judgments and will shrink away. If they hear understanding, they will expand and open to what comes next. In preparation for teaching anything then, our hearts must be in the right place.

Remember too that teaching works best when it arises out of listening. Through listening we hear what our children need to learn at any given time. Otherwise our teaching may be off base. If we don't listen deeply, even our best teaching will make little difference, for we won't have responded to what they are ready to hear.

Although children are born with wisdom and common sense they do not necessarily know how to access it. They are not born with knowledge about the situations they will encounter in life and what to do about them. They are not born with skills. All these they have to acquire and learn.

THE TEACHING PROCESS

If we want our children to learn most anything, we would be wise to do the following:

1. create the right environment for learning
2. model the behavior we want through our own actions
3. help the child gain an understanding of the issue
4. if needed, allow the child opportunities to experience the natural results of his or her behavior.

TEACHING RESPONSIBILITY

As an example of the teaching process, let's see how this might play out in trying to teach our children responsibility. Perhaps more than anything else, most parents want their kids to be responsible. How do we teach children responsibility?

Responsibility is both an understanding and a skill. It is not something a child naturally brings into the world. Yet, all children are born with the capacity (barring a very few organic difficulties) to become responsible. Thus, we need to draw this capacity out of them and teach a few things along the way.

As implied by the four steps above, responsibility is learned in four ways:

1. through creating the right environment for learning

This means bringing to life everything stated in the previous chapters of this book.

2. by modeling responsible behavior through our own actions

What we show them is what we get. Actions speak far louder than words. If we demonstrate responsibility, they can see what we want.

3. by helping the child gain an understanding of responsibility

Essentially, we want to take opportunities—in a calm, loving, caring way, when emotions are not charged but when something occurs that reminds us of responsibility— to discuss with our children what responsibility is, what it means, why it's important, what would happen if people were not responsible, and the effect on others of being responsible or not.

4. by allowing the child to experience how responsible and irresponsible actions affect one's life

A mistake often made by parents is to rely on consequences to teach. The problem is, consequences come after the fact of the behavior. Long before consequences enter the picture comes understanding. In this chapter we will concentrate on helping children gain the understanding. How do we help our children understand how their actions affect others? How do we help them know what responsible action is and what it isn't? We need to look for opportunities to help them understand it.

For example, depending on the child's age, while watching TV together, if we see someone being irresponsible we can ask our child what effect she thinks that character's behavior is having on others. We can ask if she thinks that behavior was responsible and why. We can ask how being responsible plays out in her own life. Later, if we see her engaging in irresponsible behavior we can remind her of our conversation so she can connect it to what she is doing in the moment. If we want responsibility developed, we must be committed to ensuring that this understanding comes about.

This may take patience. We can't expect our children to get it all at once. We didn't! All we have to do is bring to mind some of our behaviors when we were young to realize that it took us a while to understand responsibility.

To help our kids understand responsibility, then, we need to:

- be *creative* in helping them understand it, such as looking around for examples in ourselves, in others, and in themselves
- be *committed* to their learning it
- be *patient* while they learn it.

The world presents infinite opportunities for creative learning.

Together, we and our children could learn more about how behaviors affect others. We might even make it a game (for pre-teens), pretending we're private investigators and observing whether we think others are being responsible or not. We might observe how the differences in behaviors affect others. We could ask our children to contrast how they are affected when we parents deal with them in different ways. We could ask them to think of a time when we did something that affected them and whether they considered what we did to be responsible. We might be surprised. Then we could discuss other ways to handle it, and which way they learn best.

With this foundation of understanding, to drive it home, we can then put our actions where our mouths are. For example, when we were trying to teach Jaime responsibility and all she wanted was to be off with her friends I said to her, "I'll tell you what, Jaime, I'll trade you freedom for responsibility." So long as we were certain that she knew what it meant to be responsible in most all situations, she could have her freedom. But she had to demonstrate her understanding with actions. We had to have confidence. Jaime could understand this trade-off, and it gave her something to aspire to.

SELF-RELIANCE

At some point our children will go off into the world without us. If they are not self-reliant they will have a very difficult time.

We want to help our children understand the relationship between what they are doing, what their choices are, and their own internal satisfaction and fulfillment. We want them to be able to look at a situation, see what is in their own long-term best interests, and act accordingly.

Remember, first we want to be sure they are in the best position to listen:
- Is our rapport right, so they will want to listen?
- Are we in the right frame of mind?
- Do we know what we're talking about?

If our teaching is not getting through, chances are that one of three things is amiss: 1) the rapport has dropped; 2) we're in the wrong frame of mind; 3) we don't know what we're talking about.

Sometimes we are too quick to try to teach. We have a lot to teach our kids—from how to use a fork, to how to cross a street, to how to clean a room, to how to be responsible, to how to deal with peer pressure, to how to avoid drugs. No matter what we try to teach—no matter what we say—it is not going to be taken in, understood, accepted, taken to heart, if we don't communicate it from an open, responsive, caring frame of mind.

We want to **assume that our children want to learn.** When very young our children thirst for knowledge. They soak it up. This is their natural state. Later, inadvertently, we often take the fun out of learning. Our children do not move fast enough for us. We get upset and take it out on them. We want them to move faster or do it right at the expense of taking the time to learn it for themselves. All for expediency! Learning becomes no fun. Then school often reinforces how un-fun learning is. Sometimes it's even painful. So children lose that natural desire to learn. Still, the desire is inside them and, if something catches their fancy, automatically they become interested.

TEACHING SELF-RELIANCE THROUGH TAKING CARE OF THE HOUSEHOLD

When children act in unfathomable ways (to us) it may be because they simply have not learned all there is to know about a given situation. Consider the issue of helping out around the house, often the bane of parents' existence. Are our kids good-for-nothing-lazy bums, or have they not understood how cleaning is in their best interests? If they understood how cleaning was in their own, best interests they would naturally develop self-reliance around cleaning. Once it took hold inside their own minds we would not have to be on their backs about cleaning up, because they would be doing it for themselves.

The more children understand in their own hearts, with their own internal logic, the need for household chores and why they are important, the more likely they will do them without a struggle. If children can see household chores as fun, the more likely they will do them. This may seem like a great leap, but one key is how we parents present and teach household responsibilities, which is determined by how we ourselves see them. If we see them as a chore and drudgery we will pass that on, it becomes what our children pick up.

At some point every child wanted to help his or her parents around the house; meaning, at some point s/he did see it as fun. This means the desire is inside of them. How did we handle it? Did we inadvertently kill it in them? Did we ruin the fun of it? Did we keep getting on them for not doing something right? Then we wonder how they lost their desire.

It is never too late! We could lighten it up. We could be a team working together. We could have a feeling of camaraderie. How can we make it fun?

We could also try to appeal to their own common sense about the need for cleaning up. Why is it important anyway? Why is it important to us?

Maybe we don't really know why it is important to us. Maybe we think it's the thing to do because our parents told us it was. Is that good enough? Sure, we could probably get compliance by forcing them, but is that really what we want? Would it not be more satisfying if they did it just because they thought it was the right thing to do?

Sometimes kids may have to be jump-started. If their room is atrocious, it may be too overwhelming for them to clean. We may have to do it once for them (maybe a few times), or do it with them because it is too overwhelming, but then we can decide what we can do together to keep it that way.

Kids usually want to help out if there's a nice feeling about it, but often we're on their case, so it becomes the last thing they're usually interested in.

Also, if we want their rooms clean, is ours clean? If it's not, they won't understand what the difference is—and for good reason. Kids learn much more from what they see than from what they hear.

Do our children understand that keeping up a household is a big responsibility? Do they understand how much there is to do? Do they understand what it is like to have the work burden fall on one person if others do not share the load and live up to their commitments? Do they understand how much easier it is for everyone to share the load? Do they understand that if they mess something up after you spent hours cleaning, they will likely feel the effects of your reaction?

If they don't live up to their commitments and we're frustrated by it, we could ask for their advice about how we might resolve it. Remember, we're talking about entering into a dialogue and partnership here, not badgering them.

If our children are not keeping the house clean, we could step back, observe and listen. We could ask ourselves what our children do not understand about cleaning up. How are they seeing it? What is important to us about cleaning up?

Would they be moved by the principle of helping each other? Would they be moved by the fact that it takes longer for people to do things alone? If not, what would move them?

When they're young, we may have to show them what needs to be cleaned and how to clean it. Even if they're older we may have to show them. They may never have considered what is involved in making something clean to people's satisfaction.

For example, if we want our children to learn table manners we have to teach them the logic. Step back and watch and listen for what they don't understand. They are not born with the knowledge of why table manners are important. We may have to ask ourselves what the logic is. Do they understand that certain people are bothered by certain things, and some people get turned off when they see others eating in a way that they would call disgusting? Do they understand that if we live our lives without bothering people our lives run more smoothly? Do they understand that people are affected by what we do?

The same holds true for keeping rooms clean. What is the logic? Would the fact that clothes get wrinkled and ruined move them? Probably not. They don't often pay for their own clothes. Would it move them to know that cleaning up after oneself keeps the pace of one's life sane? Woah! A statement like that may or may not affect them, but it is often one that makes people sit up and take notice because it is not something people normally think about when considering reasons for cleaning. It often does something for the mind to enter an orderly room; it makes many people feel peaceful. Take an eight-year-old into museum or an empty church and ask what feeling he gets. Our lives get so fast-paced that cleaning up after ourselves provides automatic regulation to keep the pace of our lives more calm. I had never thought about this before I heard George Pransky say it. I then tested it on my daughter, and Jaime seemed taken aback. She had never thought about it before either. She realized its truth. After that, she seemed to have slightly less aversion to cleaning up after herself. Not that she always did, but she cleaned up more, and when she did it seemed to calm her—provided she did it in the right frame of mind. I am not suggesting that this will work, only that **we have to find logic and reasons that our children will resonate with, reasons that surprise them a little.**

We can **step back and observe what their patterns are.** If we ask our children to clean up the living room, and we find papers and books on the floor and their jackets on the couch, perhaps the kids don't have "the eyes" for what it means to clean up. They have to be taught. So we check out what they did:

"What about the papers on the floor?"

"Oh yeah."

"What about the jacket."

"Oh yeah."

They don't see it! How many times have we done the dishes and then our partner comes along and finds some caked-on food left on a dish or glass. We didn't see it, even though we were sure we cleaned it well. That's what happens with kids.

So we might say something like, "I'm going to clean up the room and I want you to tell me what to clean up. Then after I clean up, I want you to inspect it." We could even make it fun and give them inspector sheets. But our hearts have to be in right place. We might say, "Okay, together, let's find a place for everything and then get into a habit of putting things away. And if I don't put my things away, you tell me, okay?"

* * *

Cynthia Stennis, a parent and staff social worker in Dr. Roger Mills's Health Realization community improvement effort in the Homestead Gardens housing project, has her own special way of teaching the importance of household chores. She says, "We sit down together and I ask, 'What do you think has to get done? We're all in this together. We need to work out a system. How would you like to contribute?'"

If Cynthia comes home from work and finds the apartment messy she would say, "This is your house, do you want it to look like that? Show me how you want your apartment to look."

Sometimes she comes home from work and starts to go to the kitchen to cook, but her kids want her attention. She is upset because the house is messy. But she knows better than to say anything when she's upset. So she holds her tongue until her spirits rise. Then, with a half-smile on her face, she says, "You guys wouldn't clean the bathroom, but you want me to listen to you and play with you? And I guess since you're not sleeping in your bed, you want me to make up your bed. And I guess you want me to pick up your shoes, even though they're not my shoes." Cynthia knows that the more she makes light of it, the more she makes it fun, the more they can understand.

Her other options are either: 1) do everything herself to get the house the way she wants it, then get angry because she has to do everything; 2) punish her children for not doing what they're supposed to; or 3) do what many parenting courses suggest, "You can't do what you want until you've done what's expected." This last approach may be okay, but it does not promote cleaning for cleaning's sake because of the power it holds over them.

Cynthia chooses the lighthearted-but-still-get-the-point-across approach. In this way her children really understand what the issues are because it is done in a nonthreatening manner. But she puts the burden of responsibility back on them so they can check out for themselves how they would really feel to be in her shoes. It worked! Her kids became very helpful around the house.

Everyone has to find their own style that they're comfortable with.

Cynthia does the same with the issue of curfew. Cynthia's fifteen-year-old son asked, "How late can I stay out?"

She replied, "If you had a son fifteen years old, how would you feel? What would you do?"

Again, the issue gets put back on him, so it teaches him to consider the issues.

Suppose after that discussion he still comes in late?

Calmly, she says to him, "Look at the time."

He says, "I know, I won't do it again."

"Okay, well what will have to happen when you do? What would you do if it were your son?"

She wants him in the position where, if he were the parent, how would he treat his child.

TEACHING SELF RELIANCE THROUGH DISAPPOINTMENT AND BOREDOM

At a fairly early age one of the things that children need to learn is about dealing with disappointment and boredom.

If kids are disappointed about something, many of us have a tendency to try to distract them, to get them involved in something else. This is okay occasionally, but what does it teach them?

Dr. George Pransky suggests that, for the most part, it is better to let them be disappointed. If they experience that, at times, they will be disappointed, that they may not be able to have everything they want whenever they want it, they may cry in frustration, then it's over and they move on. It's no big deal. When they experience big disappointments later in life, such as the loss of a love relationship, they will not get bowled over so easily and will be able to move on. If our children are disappointed and crying, we can show them compassion about their frustration. We, too, sometimes need to learn that disappointments are part of life, that we get over them, that they're no big deal, and we move on.

Part of "self-reliance" is children learning to handle their own negative feelings and temporary setbacks.

If kids are bored, many of us have a tendency to either do something to take away their boredom, or we tell them to do something to busy themselves. Yet, if we look closely, we can see that, often, people are bored because they are too highly stimulated. They are used to running, running, having a million things to do, and then when it stops they are lost and need something to fill the void. They don't know what to do with themselves. When the stimulation stops for a few moments, boredom steps in to take its place.

MTV and the advertising industry have not helped. They flash so many images across the screen so quickly that three seconds without a change begins to seem like an eternity.

The alternative is to let kids be bored. This slows them down. "Once you quiet your mind and calm down it will occur to you what to do." Boredom is a mind going too fast. Slowing down helps us find our bearings. If we run around trying to find something else to stimulate our children with, they will need more and more stimulation to think they're happy. A lot of enjoyment can come out of a little stimulation—if we let it. Do we want to be entertaining our kids all the time, or do we want them to be entertaining themselves? Of course we want to spend quality time with our children, but we don't want to be stimulating them all the time.

Part of self-reliance is children learning to take care of their own entertainment. Often, the most beautiful moments are the most peaceful, when we deeply appreciate the little that is going on.

JUDGMENT CALLS VS. COMMON SENSE

Common sense issues and judgment issues are different issues, and we would be wise to deal with them differently.

For example, when teenagers want to go somewhere that a parent considers dangerous, there is no way to tell whether something bad will actually happen.

If a parent is concerned about whether to allow a teenager to go to a particular party, George Pransky suggests this approach, discussing it in a respectful, caring way:

"I don't know whether I'm right, but as a parent it's my job to make this decision. Some things are judgment calls. Do you agree? Do you agree that there are some things parents need to make the decision about? I don't know whether I'm right here or not, but in this case I'm not willing to take the chance to let you go."

The kid may not like it, but she's bound to respect it more than just saying, "No way! Case closed! You can't go, period." So long as the child feels really listened to, and understands that it's a tough question, and that you're doing your best, and she feels a sense of resolve about it, it will usually end up okay. People can't always reach agreement but, as Dr. Steve Glenn says, they need to feel listened to and taken seriously.

Some parents will ask, "Why should I waste my time? I'm the parent! What I say goes!" That may be true, but we have to ask ourselves what we want our kids to learn. Will he learn, "When someone bigger than you and tells you to do something, you do it!" Then suppose some big guy comes along wanting to sexually abuse him? Or what happens when he's in a situation where he can tell a smaller kid what to do? What do we really want our kids to learn?

Do we want our kids to learn, as a parent, what are the kinds of things we consider when we make decisions like this? I think so.

Of course there are times parents have the last word. Yet, if we want to have our relationships with our children prosper, and if we want them to learn how decisions are made in life and how to access their own common sense, we want to help them understand as much as possible. Where we are coming from? How do we see it? We also want to listen to what they would do, and be open enough to be affected by how they see it and have our minds changed.

The alternative is force of will and bad feelings. **Is it worth it to be right all the time and have a bad relationship?**

On the other hand, some things are just common sense. Does one go walking alone at night in a neighborhood where people have been known to be hurt, shot, or raped? That's obvious common sense. That is nonnegotiable. Kids can understand the difference between common sense and judgment calls. But first we have to be able to see the difference ourselves.

HOW DO WE KNOW WHAT KIDS NEED TO LEARN?

In sum, **it is essential to teach kids what they need to know to get along in the world. We can't leave it to chance.**

We know what kids need to learn by watching and listening carefully. If a kid is having problems with a certain issue, such as being loud when the parent is on the telephone, that becomes our signal for what he needs to learn more about. Kids need to learn many things that we take for granted. If we're too quick to get upset or to punish, or too quick to use logical consequences, we've missed an opportunity to help the child learn self-reliance.

We need to ask ourselves, "What don't they know about a situation? Why would they be acting this way?" Then, take a step back and watch with an open, clear mind. We'll usually see what they need to understand

In the telephone example, we may find that the child does not understand that we can't hear when she's making noise. Then we want to ask ourselves why it's important. Some things we think are important may not be. Not everything can be a huge issue; we have to pick our spots. In this example, we might think it is very important to be able to hear when someone is talking to us. It's respectful to the other party to be able to give them our undivided attention. We have to teach that to our child. We may have to demonstrate how it's hard to hear, so the child understands.

Once we hone in on an issue we have to stick to it, one way or another, until we come to a meeting of the minds with our children. Usually that can only happen through open dialogue. This is how learning happens, short of learning through experiencing natural consequences (letting the natural course of events unfold and make their point naturally, such as leaving a banana peel on the floor and slipping on it). Still, sometimes we cannot afford to have the natural consequence happen, as in teaching the child why she should not run out in the street.

Children below age seven are developmentally incapable of reasoning well, so we do not want to try. There, we have to take quick action. But we can still talk to them about why we're doing what we do. This sets up a pattern and should begin as early as possible, even though the child doesn't really understand what we're talking about. They pick up the tone and begin to get used to this approach.

Again, **if the most important thing to develop in a child is wisdom and common sense, we want our children to learn how to step back from a situation, see the big picture, and know the best thing to do. When a** child's mind is in a quiet, calm state, they will usually be able to find their common sense. The more secure they are, the more access they have to their wisdom.

At the same time we want to maintain rapport, but also to be sure that the child understands that we stand behind what we say. **We will stick with the issue at hand until its learned. Patiently we will ensure that it is learned.**

Children are so innocent. They can get out of control and not see how it affects other people. They need guidance from their parents to teach them how to keep their bearings, how to function when they get out of control, how "out of control" happens. When they lose control it means they're in pain. Something is wrong. They are off-kilter, and they're suffering. We are aiding them by helping them to regain their bearings. They don't like being that out of control, but they can't help it. They're doing the only thing that they know how to do. Again, if we take a step back, we can see what specifically needs to be taught, and patiently stick with it.

One caution: If we stop enjoying our children, we're doing too much teaching.

SUMMARY POINTS ABOUT TEACHING

In summary, to teach our children anything and have it stick, the following ingredients are needed:

* **Become completely grounded in the issue we want to teach about.**

We want to be crystal clear in our own minds why this issue is so important to us.

* **Be the model of what we want to teach.**
* **Be sure our hearts are in the right place.**

We want to see where we're coming from and be sure we have the proper respect and faith in our child. Can we see that our child really wants to learn and that he wants to be a productive, nice person? When we lose this view, when we think the kid doesn't mean well and is up to no good, we need to step back and recognize those feelings, then use that observation to right ourselves.

* See the big picture.

The purpose of guidance is self-reliance. We want to stimulate and resonate with their common sense, to develop their wisdom.

* Take nearly every opportunity to teach what needs to be taught, being sure we help our child see the reason why the issue is so important.

* See what it is that they don't understand that explains why they are having this difficulty.

If the child is not understanding the importance of an issue or what to do about it, we want to step back and observe and listen until we see specifically what he does not understand. For example, we want to say to ourselves, "Okay, my kid doesn't want to clean off the table. He knows how to do it. He knows we expect it. What doesn't he understand? I assume he wants to be a nice, productive person. If he really understood its importance, it would make sense to him to do that job."

We then want to step back and observe. Maybe we don't truly understand why it's so important. Maybe he doesn't understand that sometimes you have to do things that you don't want to do for the greater good. If we're stuck and can't see it, we might want to say to ourselves, "Right now I can't see what the problem is, but I'd really like to understand." Then we want to take it off our minds, but keep observing and have faith that we will eventually see what he needs.

* Reach a meeting of the minds and stay in rapport while doing so.

* Stick with it until it is learned

Sometimes this means having patience over time.

105

TEACHING RESPECT

To illustrate the above, let's walk through how I, as a parent, would want to teach my own child respect. What process would I go through?

The first thing I would want to ask myself is, "Why do I care about respect? Why is respect important to me?"

The reason may be different for each of us. For me, I would say respect is important because it is the essence of people getting along in the world. Without respect we would have disrespect. People then would think they had license to walk all over anyone at any time. People would get hurt. There would be chaos.

Does this explanation satisfy me? Do I feel grounded in it? Pretty much, but it feels like I'm missing something. Respect is also something that one needs for oneself. People who don't have respect for themselves don't care, and when people don't care they tend to harm themselves and others.

This feels closer. Maybe I should look up "respect" in the dictionary to perhaps give me more of an insight.

The American Heritage Dictionary says that "to respect" means, "1. to feel or show esteem for, to honor." Wow! That's nice. Respect is the basis for esteem. Respect means honoring people. Imagine how peaceful, how beautiful the world would be if everyone honored everyone else!

What else does it say? "2. to show consideration for; avoid violation of; treat with deference." Again, wouldn't the world be a wonderful place to live if we each took it upon ourselves to be considerate of other human beings and their property and avoided violating them in every way. That's how I would want to live!

What would we have if we didn't have respect? The antonym of respect is, "abuse; misuse; scorn." Which world would we rather live in? I know where I stand. I sure would rather be honored than abused. If I want that for me, then I ought to be willing to give that to others. That goes for my children, too. In fact, it is really important to me that they be that way. I would like them to live in such a world, and it begins at home.

Now I feel well-grounded in why respect is so important to me, and why I want my children to learn it.

I then want to take every opportunity I can find (without being obnoxious about it) to be sure that they learn it.

First, I want to be sure that I continually show them respect, even when I am angry with them. If I am so caught up in my own thinking or mood that I blow it and do not show respect, I want to go back and apologize. I want to let them know how I realize I was not showing respect, and why that was wrong. If I want to teach them respect, I want to be the model of it—from their perspective.

For example, if I want them to respect my belongings, to take care of them, to not get into my things, I can't get into their things. If I break something of theirs by accident I'm responsible for replacing it. Again, if I yell at them, I am not honoring them, so I have to watch myself and apologize if I slip. I have to get myself in order first.

Next, to teach respect I want to begin at the earliest possible time, when they are very young, when they are first able to comprehend. [Note: Some of you will be reading this when your kids are already teenagers. It is never too late! It is just easier the younger that they are. Teenagers often seem to forget what they learned when they were younger anyway.]

In this case, teaching at the earliest time means when toddlers first begin to interact with others. When I see my little boy yank a toy out of his little sister's hands, I might want to say, "Honey, it's not okay for you to take something from someone." I'm not saying that he's bad. I'm not saying that he's not nice. I'm not judging him. I'm just stating a fact: It's not okay.

When he gets a little older, say, ages four to six, and we're reading a book or watching TV together and a character does something that smacks of disrespect, I might say, "Do you think that man was being nice?" After he answers I might add, "I don't think he was being nice [either]. That's called 'disrespect.' That's something that we don't do in this family. We always try to show respect." At this point all I want to do is to plant this seed: Here's the difference between respect and disrespect, and our family comes down on the side of respect.

At around age six or seven when he can defer gratification for at least a couple of minutes I might say, "When you see someone on TV do something that doesn't show respect, come and get me so we can talk about it." Or, "When someone does something at school that doesn't show respect, come and tell me about it when I get home."

All this is preliminary seed-planting, letting him know what I expect. Most of my teaching will come when I see him either showing or not showing respect.

If I observe that he has just shown respect in some way, I want to point out how much I appreciate it and why. "Thanks for showing respect. It makes the world a really nice place to live in."

When he does not show respect, that is a signal to me that we have more teaching to do. In this case, I want to ask myself a few questions:

- "Does he understand what respect is?"
- "Does he understand why respect is important?
- "Does he understand what I expect about showing respect?"

As an eight-year-old he just knocked over his six-year-old sister. Here is a hypothetical dialogue:

"Eric, was that showing respect?"

"I don't know."

"Well, tell me what you think respect is."

"I don't know."

"Okay, if you don't remember, that explains the problem. Let's explore what respect is. What does respect mean to you?"

"I don't know."

"Okay, tell me how you like to be treated."

"I don't know."

"If you don't know, that means I could treat you in any way I could think up and it wouldn't matter to you, right?"

[Seeing it coming.] "Well, maybe not any way."

"Oh, so maybe you do like some ways better than other ways."

"Well, I don't like to be yelled at or hit."

"Neither do I. Would you say that was respect?"

"I guess not."

"Well, what about if you yell or push your little sister? Would you say that was respect?"

"She took my ball!"

"That's not what I asked. But since you brought it up, would you say that was she did was respectful?"

"No!"

"Okay, it wasn't! Now, would you say that what you did to her in return was respectful?"

"How come you're not talking to her then?"

"Because right now I'm talking to you. I didn't know she took your ball. After we talk I'll have a talk with her, but right now all we're talking about is whether you understand what respect means."

"I do."

"Tell me what you think it means."

"It means not hitting."

"It means that to me too. Anything else?"

"That's about it."

"What about if some big guy came along and pushed you down. Would that be respect?"

"No."

"What about when you push down your little sister?"

"I guess not. But she took my ball."

"Okay, do you think there might be a way to handle it where you would still show respect?"

"I don't know. I guess I could ask her for it nicely."

110

"That sounds respectful. And what if she still didn't give it back. How would you still show respect?"

"I could tell you."

"That's one approach. It sounds like you understand what respect means now. Okay, thanks for the talk. I love you."

Now, I don't kid myself. Just because we've had this conversation does not mean that from then on he will show respect in every situation. But at least I know now that he knows what respect means. He may not have given me a very eloquent definition, he may not have covered all bases, he may forget later, but he was able to contrast respect and disrespect in terms of how he would act, and that's what counts for now.

The next time the issue of respect comes up I want to be on it again. As important as respect is to me, I never want there to be a time where if he is disrespectful I let it go by, although if he or I are in a low moods I may want to say, "We'll talk about this later."

At age twelve I might overhear him talking back to his mother.

"Eric, is that showing respect?"

"I don't know."

"You've told me before that you don't feel respected if somebody yells at you. What about if someone talks back to you?"

"I don't know."

"Would you like it if I talked back to you?"

"I don't care."

"Really? So you mean it's okay if I start talking back to you?"

"If that's what turns you on."

"I wouldn't do it because I don't think it's respectful. Ask your mother how it made her feel when you talked back to her."

111

"I don't want to."

"So you must think it's not so good, otherwise you would have no problem asking."

Silence.

"Look, kiddo, I'm not mad at you. I'm not upset. But I think you hurt your mother's feelings and, to me, when you hurt someone else's feelings, especially your own mother, that's not showing respect. It's no different than hurting someone with your fists. It still hurts. And hurting someone in any way is not respect. Being respectful is really important to me. So when you feel up to it, why don't you apologize to your mother for not being respectful, okay?"

Here, I'm educating him a little more about some of the finer points of respect. I can tell from his tone that he's in a low mood, so I don't want to push any more at this time. But I also want to be sure that he is clear what is included within the definition of respect, and that it's so important to me I'm not going to let him off the hook.

Now, suppose we had that conversation and he keeps talking back. Then I've got to start asking myself, "Let's see. He understands what respect is, at least that talking back is not respect. He understands—at least I think he does—how important it is to me. What could be going on here?"

This assumes we have a good relationship, that we have followed what preceded this chapter of this book. I want to assume that it is not defiance. I want to give him the benefit of the doubt. If so, I become very curious. There must be something about respect that he doesn't understand or he wouldn't be doing what he is doing. I wonder if doesn't understand for himself what is so important about it. Maybe he doesn't see the importance of it as I do.

Suppose he's fifteen.

"Eric, I'm really puzzled. Usually, you do what I ask. But we've talked before about how important respect is and how talking back isn't respect, and you're still doing it. What's going on?"

"She's so stupid sometimes."

"That's an excuse not to show her respect?"

Silence.

"Why do you think I care about this so much?"

"I don't have the foggiest idea, dad. Why don't you tell me. You always do."

"No, I don't think I want to right now. I can tell by your tone that you look upon this whole thing with disdain. I'm really puzzled by this. I don't understand, and I was hoping you could help me out here. But I'll tell you what, we never have to bring it up again if you just treat her—all of us—with respect. Okay? Think about it."

Then I want to step back and observe.

I might notice that he doesn't treat his mother with disrespect all the time. Under what circumstances does he not? I might discover that what he said is true: he only doesn't treat her with respect if he thinks she says or does something stupid. Then he treats her like dirt, as if that somehow makes it okay to treat her with disrespect. At such times he either doesn't see the connection, or his own feelings override it. So when he's in reasonably good spirits—perhaps when we're doing something nice alone together (so long as it doesn't ruin the moment)—I want to help him understand what he doesn't appear to understand.

"Eric, I noticed that you were right. Pretty much the only time you don't treat your mother with respect is when you think she does something that you would call stupid."

"Yeah."

[Note: I could go in many directions with this one, but I'm choosing to deal with it at the level of respect.] "

"It looks to me like you think, if she acts stupid that's a license for all the rules of respect to go out the window. Is that true?"

"Well, no, dad. Not really."

"Then I'd really like to understand."

"It's not that I think it's right. It's just that she makes me so frustrated. Then I forget."

[Note: There are lots of meaty issues here, such as Eric thinking that someone makes him feel a certain way, instead of it coming from his own thinking. If I could help him understand how he is the source of his own feelings through his own thinking, he would be less frustrated by his mother's actions. But I want to file that one away for another day because, right now, the main issue is respect, and I don't want to lose the thread.]

"Oh, I think I understand. So you're saying that you don't think it's right at those times, but you can't help yourself. You lose yourself in the moment."

"Yeah."

"Oh, okay, I can relate to that. Sometimes I lose myself in the moment too. Everyone does. The one problem is, she's still feeling disrespected."

Silence.

"Got any ideas about that?"

"Not really, dad."

"Well, if someone got really upset with you because he thought that you did something stupid and he punched you out, would it be okay if they just lost themselves in the moment?"

"I would never do anything stupid."

"Well, suppose someone else thinks you did, even if you don't think so. Would it be okay?"

"No."

"What would you want from them instead?"

"Well, they'd have to do more than just apologize later. I don't want them to hit me in the first place."

"What would you want them to do?

"To tell me about it, tell me what I supposedly did wrong.

"How would you want them to tell you."

"Nicely."

"So even though they've gotten lost in their emotions you still want them to do that?"

"Yeah, they could wait until they calmed down."

"Do you think the same could hold true for your mother."

Silence. "I guess so."

"Okay, all I want you to do is watch yourself when you get that way. Just see yourself. Become aware of it, okay?"

"Okay, I'll try."

"And if you find it too hard, come and talk to me, and maybe we can come up with some ideas about some other ways to look at this. Okay, kiddo?"

By seeing it in himself, instead of my coming down on him, I'm trying to get his own common sense to kick in. When it does—when he truly understands its importance—I know that he will naturally show respect. I have to keep helping him see its importance—until he does.

Or, I could have just sent him to his room for being disrespectful, but we would have missed all those opportunities for learning about respect that he will be able to draw upon in the future. Ultimately, I want him self-reliant about the issue of respect

REVERSING THE LOGIC

Midway through her sophomore in high school, Jaime's grades plummeted. She had been hanging out at a park with a bunch of kids who at best lacked direction and at worst were taking drugs and being a bad influence. Yet, she had begun to gravitate toward a new group of friends who were very highly motivated and were excellent students. We

115

were thankful about her new choice of friends, but Jaime had not yet taken on their work ethic. She wanted simply to hang around them. Yet, a 67 appeared on her report card. Her mother confronted her.

In response Jaime became sarcastic and snapped, "Well, I know I'm disappointing you. I know that I'm a big disappointment in your life because I'm failing. You think I'm a failure. You just think I'm a failure because I'm not as good as you, and I'm not you. Well, I'm who I am, and I'm not David, and I'm not you. Well, fine, I'm a failure!"

Judy looked at her. She knew that Jaime was really disappointed in herself. She knew that Jaime didn't want to bring home a report card that she wasn't proud of. Judy knew that Jaime was capable of a lot more than that, dyslexia or not.

Judy then came out with one of the all-time great lines: "No, honey, you're not a big disappointment in my life. I don't feel like you're a failure. As a matter of fact, I think that if this is what you want for your life—if you don't want to go to college, or if you want to go to a second-rate school, or not go to the school of your choice—whatever it is that you want to do—I think you're succeeding at it admirably. Because you're doing all the things that will keep you from going anywhere in your life. No, I don't think you're a failure. I think you're an enormous success. I think you're doing a wonderful job because you're going to get exactly what you've got your sights on."

For the first time in her life, Jaime didn't answer back. She was speechless. Judy had stopped her dead in her tracks. She had turned the tables on her.

Jaime had all kinds of dreams about going to a good, progressive college. She suddenly realized that if she kept on this track she wouldn't get there. From that moment on, Jaime did a complete turnaround in school. She had been in standard classes, surrounded by unmotivated students. At the beginning of her junior year she petitioned the school to let her into accelerated classes (where her new friends were). No one in the school but her guidance counselor supported her. They didn't think she could make the grade. But Jaime knew she could and persisted. She finally prevailed. In her senior year, in accelerated classes, she earned high honors.

Judy had turned her around, not by telling Jaime what she wasn't doing right, force butting against force, but by joining with Jaime's force and, as in the martial art of Aikido, depositing it elsewhere.

I never would have come up with a line like that, but the great teacher/schoolmaster Marva Collins has. To reach her unmotivated or problem students she has been known to say [paraphrased], "I see your image. Is this what you'd really like to be in ten years? If not, what are you doing now to be where you want in ten years? Whatever you decide to be is your choice. You don't have to be here. In the streets nothing is demanded of you. Pick the box you'd like to live in. Pick the corner you'd like to hang on. And that's a blessing. A lot of people don't know what they want to do."

It's hard to escape this kind of reverse logic. When people truly see what they're doing to themselves, there's no escape. When people see the thinking that is driving them to nowhere, or driving them to destruction, there's nowhere to run and nowhere to hide. This is when learning takes hold most.

OUR CHILDREN GROW UP AND HIT THE ROAD

The day my son graduated from high school, I suddenly wondered whether I had prepared him well enough for life.

In a few days he would leave for the summer and then for college. He would be on his own. How will he do out there in the world? Did I prepare him well enough? Will he be okay without us?

It is a sad day. I'm not ready for him to go. I love him very much.

It is also a happy day—a day of gratitude.

Given the world we live in today, and given the little I thought I knew as a parent, I thank my lucky stars every day that he came out of high school not abusing alcohol or other drugs much beyond experimentation, not getting anyone pregnant or contracting HIV, not being violent or a delinquent, not being depressed or suicidal, not being too unmanageable for his parents to handle. On top of that, he did well in school. He worked hard. He excels at basketball. He has many friends, both male and female. I thank my lucky stars.

But is he happy? I sometimes wonder. I think so, but he's rather moody, especially when he wakes up in the morning. But he's a teenager. And he had much to overcome.

When he was in the fourth grade he suffered a cerebral hemorrhage and nearly died. After major brain surgery we learned that it diminished his learning capability, that he could no longer read well, that he could no longer spell, that he couldn't find words for things he knew. He plummeted from among the top of his class.

But he never wanted to be different. For a year he had to play basketball with a boxing helmet. He refused Special Education. He worked so hard to regain his learning ability. And it worked. He did! On his own! No one can know what he went through. I'm so proud of him.

Yet we also learned that he had bleeding into the frontal lobe of his brain, and that is where behavior is controlled. We were told that, especially during his teenage years when all those hormones were kicking around, from time to time that scar tissue would get irritated, and when it did, once it reached a certain level, he wouldn't be able to control his behavior. They were right!

He peaked in obnoxiousness at age fifteen. He was difficult for us to handle. Thank God for what we learned from Dr. Steve Glenn and his parenting course, *Developing Capable People* [See Appendix]. We became fairly practiced at catching problem situations as soon as they were beginning to escalate—because once his scar tissue became irritated and it escalated beyond a certain point, there was no stopping him.

It was still hard. Home was where he felt safest; therefore home was where he let off most steam. During much of that year I can't say we had a very good relationship with him. Things were strained much of the time.

Toward the end of that year, serendipitously, I heard that tape by Darlene and Charles Stewart cited in Chapter 1. When Darlene said that no matter what horrible, crazy things her teenager did, she would stop trying to control him and just love him, "even if that meant bringing him cookies in jail," it changed my approach. I backed off and just tried to have a good time with him.

Yes, the relationships with our children matter most, but I found myself wondering if my son had learned enough from me, whether he was prepared. So what do I want him to have learned as I send him on his way, off on his own? What do I want him to understand about life? What will help guide him through any difficult times? If I could only just tell him.

Hey, wait! I can!

Here is what I want him to know; some words of wisdom that will guide him reasonably happily through life.

"Always know that—

* No matter what happens to you in life—no matter what ups and downs life may bring—you have all the health and well-being inside you that you will ever need, it can never be destroyed, and it contains the wisdom and common sense to guide you through life.

* All you need to do to hear it is to quiet your mind or clear your head (which you can do in any way that suits you), and it will speak to you in the form of common sense thoughts popping into your head—so all you need to do is trust that it's there.

* When you feel frustrated or angry or irritable or down or bored or lazy, or any of those emotions, the more you know that those feelings are coming from your own thoughts, and those thoughts are coming only from the way you're seeing things at the moment—and that can change— the less you will be controlled by those emotions. The more you notice and are aware of what you're feeling at those times and the less you take those thoughts too seriously because those thoughts are just tricking you by giving you faulty messages, the less you will be controlled by those emotions. The more you can't let go of something, the further away you are from that health, but you're the one making it up—inadvertently.

* The more you understand that everyone sees the world in a completely different way from everyone else because of their own way of thinking, and their world makes as much sense to them as yours does to you, and you can't talk anyone out of their world any more than they can talk you out of yours, the less you will be bothered and troubled by others.

* The more you recognize your moods, and that you think differently about the same situation depending on your moods, and the more you wait until your mood rises

before acting or saying anything, the better off you'll be and the better people will respond to you.

* If someone does you wrong or treats you badly—including a basketball coach—it's just that he's lost—his world is telling him to act that way, and he is just doing the best he knows how to do at the time, given how he sees things. If you can see him as innocent because he can't see a better way at that time, and if you see him with compassion because he must be hurting to be taking it out on you, and if you don't take what they do or say personally, you will be protected emotionally from what he and others do. [Note: This does not mean not taking appropriate action, when necessary.]

* Whenever you're down in the dumps or caught up in your emotions and you can't seem to change your thinking, all you need to remember is that your thoughts will eventually change and, with them, you will see your situation or that person differently. What you see as "reality" or "the way it is" now will change as your thinking changes—and it always does. So you don't have to get so caught up in the way you think it is now—because how it looks now is guaranteed to change, eventually.

* The way you treat others creates what you get back in return.

* People who achieve what they want in life believe they can do it, trust that what they want will fall into place for them, if they work hard to get it and don't give up. And if it doesn't work out, have faith that you will be okay—it is all unfolding perfectly—no matter what.

* We will always be there for you if you need us.

* We will always love you no matter what you do!"

IX. SETTING LIMITS, AND DISCIPLINE

Up to now, this may seem like a pretty laissez-faire approach to parenting. Not so! Kids need limits! They may not like the limits at the time, but in the long run they appreciate them.

Discipline is the last chapter of this book for an important reason. Without the lessons of all previous chapters, disciplining children can cause detrimental results.

Let's put discipline in context.

THE MEANING OF DISCIPLINE

Most of us have lost sight about what the word "discipline" means. It comes from the Latin word, "disciplina," meaning, "instruction" or "knowledge." Most parents think of discipline as either punishment or consequences. Without teaching, however, discipline is off base. **The purpose of discipline is not to punish; its purpose is for children to learn.**

This means that everything in the previous chapter about teaching is really what discipline should be about. Nearly always, teaching should be applied before attempting to use any consequences.

BEFORE DISCIPLINE

The preliminaries to teaching, then, are also the preliminaries of discipline. To repeat them in this context:

* access our wisdom and common sense

When we do not have access to our wisdom and
common sense it is not time to discipline. When angry and
upset we do not want to discipline. We want a calm frame
of mind. Sometimes our children will misbehave in ways
that make us want to bring our wrath down upon them. At
those times we are just dying to punish right then and there.
Barring an emergency, though, it is always best to first get
over our anger or our bother. So long as we're bothered by
what our children are doing we will not act the way we
would if we had perspective. When upset, we may do
something we'll regret because we're not thinking right.
Instead, we want to step back, observe and reflect, and look
for the best answer before disciplining.

* see troublesome behavior as acts of insecurity

Let's say a kid goes to school stoned, is extremely
disruptive, threatens his teachers, pushes drugs, brings a
gun to school, and beats up other kids. His behaviors are
the least of the problem. Sure, they're huge problems, but
there is a much larger one. Imagine how troubled and lost
and fearful and insecure this teenager must be to have to do
such outrageous things to get by in life. In disciplining,
then, the "troubledness" becomes the focus. This does not
mean we shouldn't take responsibility to protect others, or
to uphold laws and rules. The kid must be held accountable
and cannot be let off the hook. If we want this kid to
change, however, we must see the troubledness. This will
cause our discipline to be conducted with compassion,
which may allow an opening to get through to him.
Otherwise, we don't stand a chance.

* insist on rapport, and be in a secure, responsive state

When conducted in an atmosphere of closeness and calmness, discipline has more power. Nothing is more powerful than taking a firm, unmoving stand without being upset. Nothing is more powerful than being firm, calm and reasonable. If our kids think we are unfair, or if they hate us at the time, or if they see that our own anger or upset is driving our actions, they then have an excuse to blame whatever is happening on something outside of themselves. Within an atmosphere of closeness, calmness and firmness, there is nothing left to blame. They are forced to look only at themselves. As has been suggested repeatedly, when kids sense a bad feeling on our part, they automatically kick into "damage control" to protect themselves. This is why some kids try to get away as fast as possible, why others talk back, why some tune out, why some storm out of the room, or whatever they do. All are for the purpose of avoiding the emotion emanating from us and to protect themselves. Just as our children are experts at picking up our feeling, we need to become experts at knowing immediately when something is not right with our feeling. The feeling is our compass. It tells us whether we're on track.

THE PURPOSE OF DISCIPLINE

What would we like our discipline to accomplish?

As parents, we would be wise to ask ourselves a very important question: Do we want our children to do what is right because they fear getting punished, or to do what is right because they are internally motivated to do what's right?

The choice is ours.

Every time we experience a problem with our children's behavior we are at a fork in the road. We can walk down one of two paths:

1) the moving-toward-well-being path

2) the moving-away-from-pain path

Through which path would we rather have our children motivated?

Children who grow up in an environment where parents mostly react to their "bad" behaviors tend to behave out of fear or to avoid pain. They understand little else. Such children tend to become either compliant or resistant. They find little motivation from within. They learn to react to things outside themselves.

Children who grow up in a secure environment where parents generally help them to look at a situation and learn from it tend to seek their own sense of well-being and happiness. Such an approach brings out their natural healthy tendencies. These children tend to be internally motivated to do what's right out of their own common sense.

Simply being aware of this helps gauge our direction.

Some parents will say, "If my parents told me to do something and I didn't do it, I'd get a beating, and you can bet I did it then! What worked for me should be good enough for them!"

Again, we have to ask ourselves whether we want our kids to behave because they are running scared or because they see that it is in their own long-term best interests to behave well.

True, so long as we are bigger than our kids, by sheer force we can get them to do what we want. Unfortunately this approach contains a few flaws. First, we can only get them to do something by force when we're around them, and we are not around twenty-four hours a day. If kids learn to behave because someone is forcing them, when no force or controls are present, they may tend to misbehave, for there would be no reason not to. Second, we may not always be bigger than they are. Third, they will be learning that when someone is bigger than you, he can make you do whatever he wants, so if they find someone smaller they will likely return the favor. Fourth, they won't be learning why certain things are right and wrong to apply that learning to similar situations.

If force won't work to the extent we may like, what will?

TAKING CHARGE

In her senior year of high school our daughter Jaime contracted mononucleosis. She had been on the run, burning the candle at both ends, and it all caught up with her. She was barely able to move for about a week, then was too sick to attend school for about two weeks after that—a lot of school lost.

As kids are wont to do (not to mention many adults), as soon as she started feeling somewhat better she wanted to be out running around again. Judy and I saw it coming. In this situation we knew more than Jaime did. We knew that mono stays in the system for quite some time and, during the recovery period, if a teenager overdoes it, s/he can relapse badly. We told her; it didn't move her. It was far more important to go to a party with her friends that night. She started to argue with us. All her friends were outside encouraging her to come.

Judy told her, "No! I'm not letting you do this!"

Jaime came running to me. "It's not fair!"

I said, "No, mom is absolutely right. This is where we're drawing the line."

Jaime became enraged.

We said, "Sorry, honey, this is what we think we have to do."

Begrudgingly and angrily, she stayed home.

When issues are really important to parents, parents simply have to draw the line. Young kids don't understand danger. Teenagers will place having a good time in the present above anything else. God knows, we don't want to kill their enthusiasm for having a good time in the moment—we could use a lot more of that in our own lives—but we have to draw the line at what we consider really important.

128

As Dr. Steve Glenn says, **we can draw the line with firmness (if we say it, we mean it), dignity (not doing it in a way that will embarrass them or put them down), and respect (say it with kindness and caring).** Where we can, it is best to involve children in determining what is appropriate and inappropriate. Sometimes that is not possible.

Sometimes parents simply need to step in and take charge, but it must feel right in the moment. It must come from a clear head as opposed to a feeling of desperation. There is a huge difference.

One night as I was walking up the street toward the house I heard yelling and screaming coming from inside my house. It sounded terrible. I ran in to find my seventeen-year-old son practically beating on my fifteen-year-old daughter. It apparently had something ridiculous to do with wanting to watch different programs on TV. David, who is larger than all of us, controlled the situation, refusing to watch anything but what he wanted to watch, refusing to move to his bedroom to watch his own TV, refusing to let my daughter into his room to watch his TV because she always messed up his room. In short, he was in a mighty low mood.

So was his mother, who was threatening to rip our son's cable box right out of the TV. One more time I was the one with the fresh perspective. [Note: Judy will have to be the one to write about all the times she's bailed me out when I've been the one caught up; for some reason I can't remember those as well.] By this time you know why I had perspective: I was not in the middle of it. Instinctively I knew I needed to take charge. I quickly assessed the situation to see whether calm enough heads could prevail to hear what I was going to say, despite high emotions.

I said to David, "Look, this can't happen here! You know this. [We had talked about it many times in the past but hadn't had the need for at least six months]. I don't think taking away the cable box is going to solve the problem. From now on, here's what's going to happen. If you can't agree on what program to watch down here in the den, then you've got two choices: 1) Either you let her watch what she wants down here, and you go up to your room to watch, or 2) you let her up in your room to watch. You're the one with the extra TV. Does that make sense?"

No one could find any reason it didn't make sense. Even my son saw the common sense logic to it, even though he didn't like it.

"Okay, so we agree?"

I made sure that each said they agreed. If anyone tried to bring up something extraneous to the agreement, I cut them off.

"We're just talking about this right now. That's irrelevant to this discussion."

I got an agreement.

"Secondly, Dave, you know you can't beat on her. You're much bigger than she is, and she could get hurt. I know you don't intentionally try to hurt her, but when you start doing that and people start getting wild, people can get hurt unintentionally—sometimes very badly! It just doesn't make sense to put people in that kind of danger, does it? I mean, think about it. What if something really terrible happened, and you didn't mean it?"

My intent was to get him to tap into his common sense—for himself. I didn't want him to not do it because I said so, or for Judy, or even for Jaime's safety. I wanted him to see for himself, deep down inside, "it really isn't a good idea for me to potentially cause damage to somebody, especially to someone I love, even though I hate her sometimes." I wanted him to see the logic for himself. I saw something click within him, so nothing else needed to be said at that moment.

If he hadn't seen the logic and started arguing with me, or started making excuses, or was too overwrought to deal sensibly at that time, I would have said, "We'll talk about this later." Then when emotions had cooled I'd try any way I could think of to get it to connect with him. I may find that he's too close to the situation to hear it, so I may have to draw inferences to a friend, or to myself when I was young, or to someone else with a different but similar problem. Sometimes it is best to teach impersonally so that no perceived threat can impede learning. Ultimately, I am committed to help him see it, in whatever way I can.

If I had simply punished him I would be sending my son down the avoid-pain-and-fear path. He would be careful around his little sister—when he saw me coming. Or, I could try to help him see what is in his own long-term best interests. I wanted the latter path. I wanted to educate him about his choices for his own long-term happiness and satisfaction.

We want kids to do things because they understand, not because of a reaction to control. If we know that everyone has the wisdom and common sense in them to do what is in their best interests, wouldn't we want to help them tap into this wisdom and common sense? This is the key.

How do we know that they have wisdom and common sense in them?

Remember our first premise in chapter one? Wisdom and common sense is part of the whole package. We are born with it. It never goes away. We forget we have it, but we can tap it. So long as we back off enough to allow our emotions to die down, to relax, to clear our heads and regain our bearings, the wise, common sense thing to do will occur to us. Remember, when we come upon any problem, we want to step back and observe and keep our mouths shut. This disengages us from our emotions, provides an objective view, and engages our common sense. Our common sense then guides us to do what is best.

In the above example with my kids and the TV it may appear that I violated this point. Not so! For some reason I felt very calm, so I knew I had presence of mind enough to act. It felt right. That doesn't often happen to me. More often, I need time.

As Roger Mills says, **the point of discipline is to help children regain their perspective so they can engage their own common sense.**

DRAWING THE LINE

Suppose a sixteen-year-old wants to borrow the car. The last time he borrowed it he left it with a thimbleful of gas.

What do we want to accomplish here? If I let him borrow the car now he will learn nothing. If I prohibit it without giving a reason he will learn nothing.

So I might say something like, "No, kiddo. I'm not willing to let you borrow the car when you leave it without gas. When you do that, I might get stuck. That doesn't make any sense to me. Sorry."

"Gee dad, I'm sorry. I won't do it again."

"I appreciate that, I really do, but when you started to borrow this car I told you that you needed to be sure to bring it home with enough gas, and you said, 'Okay.'"

"Dad, I forgot. I'm sorry. Look, I really need to get to my friend's house. He's waiting for me."

"I'd love to let you take the car, but I'm not confident enough that you'll do what I ask. Maybe next time."

He may go off the wall, but that's got nothing to do with me. My job is to let him know that I mean business here. If he wants the car in the future, he'll do what I expect. It's not punishment. It's not even stated as a consequence. It's just logical on my part.

In this situation, I may or may not let him take the car, but if I do I will need an agreement of expectations beforehand, and I need confidence that it will be carried out. See, I'm not trying to prove a point. I'm only trying to ensure that, if he's going to have access to a lethal weapon to drive around in, I must have complete confidence that he's doing what's right. My getting stuck without gas is the least of the problem. With such a dangerous weapon, if he forgets other things, he could kill himself or others. How will he show me with deeds—not words–that he is responsible enough to have a car in his hands?

Teenagers often love to speed, sometimes to drink and drive. Nothing could be more dangerous! I need confidence that he's not putting himself and others in danger. I need absolute faith and trust that, if he has the car, he will not engage in these activities. Until I have this confidence, case closed! I'm not willing to take the risk. In telling him this, I need to be friendly and calm, but firm.

My confidence begins with having enough gas in the car. Through the gas issue he has to learn how important this responsibility is. If I can't trust him about gasoline, how can I be sure that I trust him about anything involving the car? So he can't use it until he gives me reason to trust. There is no need to be angry. It is merely a statement of fact.

The same holds true for staying out at night. I have to have trust that he is okay. I have to have trust that my daughter is okay. I don't want to be staying up late worrying about whether they're safe. If they want to go out they need to respect my need to trust them in that situation.

"I'll be okay, dad. There's no need to worry," won't wash. I need to be shown with deeds. Otherwise, as young teenagers, they can't go out. As older teenagers they can make their own decisions, but I still need to be able to trust. I'll even give them the benefit of the doubt, but how will they give me confidence? It's really up to them. If they know what's expected, they can decide what to do within those boundaries. We may have to have some long talks until I am sure they understand and respect it. If they betray that trust, I'm not willing to take the risk—not for punishment, not for consequences, but because of common sense.

In most parenting courses the emphasis is on the consequence. Here, the emphasis is on the logic. I want my kid to see the common sense of it as I do—or to show me something else that makes even more sense.

Somewhere within *every* situation that arises, a common sense solution exists. We parents need only to step back and find it. Then we have to help our kids find it for themselves. If our discipline is not common sense, we have to question what we're trying to accomplish.

RULES AND PUNISHMENT?

What if a child does something dreadfully wrong, is it not appropriate to punish?

The dictionary defines "punishment" as "subjecting someone to penalty for a crime, fault, or misbehavior."

If someone commits a crime (and gets caught) they have to pay a penalty. That's logical. The laws of the land define unacceptable behavior. Whether anyone likes the laws or not, when people know the general punishments for violations, they make their own decisions about obeying those laws. Few people are surprised if they break a law and then get punished. That is common sense.

Families don't have laws. Many families have rules. Do rules fall in the same category as laws?

If everyone operated out of his or her own higher wisdom, so to speak, rules would be unnecessary. Family members would automatically respect each other, not put themselves or others in danger, and generally do what is right. If I had my way I would want my family to operate like that. In growing up, however, children may not share my logic. They may not always be in touch with their common sense. Are rules then necessary?

Each family must decide this for themselves. The question is, who decides what the rules are, and who decides what should happen if rules get broken?

Most families find that when children participate in creating the household rules (if rules are deemed necessary) they take more personal responsibility for following them. To create rules together everyone in the family must take time to truly understand each other's logic and reach a meeting of the minds about what is best. If a rule is not working, the parent would be ill-advised to change it on the spot. Later it can be changed through the same process that created it.

If rules are deemed necessary, it is best if they are broad and general, and few. Here are some examples:

- We will respect other people and their property.
- We will not put ourselves or others in danger.
- We will share responsibilities to keep the household running smoothly.

Rather than call these "rules," some parents would rather call them "expectations." Some would call them "agreements. "Here is what we expect from you." In either case, everyone needs to understand what each of these means so that everyone in the household has a similar understanding. Each needs to be discussed in detail. We can make up situations and talk about whether or not they violate the rules.

135

Then, if one child hits another, we could say, "We have a rule that we will respect each other here. Is what you did respect?"

Does this mean we have to punish, to give penalty? Why would it be necessary? All we really want is for our children to understand what respect is, and to stick with it until it becomes part of them. This is the teaching part of discipline.

Only if they defiantly violate a rule would we want to consider going the next step. **The next step is to demonstrate what we will and won't tolerate. Only then might we consider having what they want to do be dependent on right action.**

Whatever happens in response to a rule violation must be logical from the point of view of the child. If a child does not do her homework, common sense dictates that she might get bad grades. Suppose we decide to withhold meals? Most of us would never do that because it is completely illogical! Suppose we decide to withhold TV? That is not logical either—unless the child watches TV when she needs to be doing her homework, and it is the reason that homework is not getting done. We can help the child make this connection to her common sense.

Suppose, however, that the child doesn't care about grades. Should the parent step in? How much does the parent care about grades?

One approach might be to say something like, "I want you to do your best. It makes life so much more enjoyable to put your whole heart and soul into whatever you're doing at the time. If you get into the habit of doing it, for the rest of your life you'll find enjoyment in whatever you're doing. If you get into the habit of taking responsibility for what you have to do, you will likely take responsibility for the rest of your life. If you do well, more opportunities are open for you. For those reasons I want you to do well. I know you have it in you. I know you can do it. I have complete confidence in you. I'm willing to give you all the support and encouragement I can, but in the long run it's your life. You have to decide for yourself what's important to you and what you want."

Another approach is to clearly state expectations: "I expect you to do your best. I expect you to do well. I know you can do it, and I will do everything I can to help you."

Either approach is okay. Neither is punitive. Both are clear. Parents should use whichever they can get behind and whichever will work best with their own kids.

Still another approach is to punish. Suppose I don't let her go out and play with her friends until she gets better grades. As with all punishment, the problem is that she may resent it and rebel. On the other hand, there is something to be said about fulfilling obligations before going out. On the other hand, going out to have fun might be what the child needs to clear her head, and then come back to the work with fresh, renewed energy. Which do we want? Parents need to decide where they come down on each issue, then help the child to see the common sense behind their own view. Parents also need to be open to the child's logic. They may learn something.

If I have to resort to punishment to get my children to do something such as homework, I am losing the battle. I shouldn't be in a battle to begin with. I want them to see how doing well is in their own long-term best interests for their own sakes.

USING LIMITS AS AN OPPORTUNITY TO DISCIPLINE (TEACH)

Dr. George Pransky says that having children reckon with limits can help them learn how to handle their own emotional upsets. Suppose a child does not want to go to bed. She gets upset. She becomes all riled up which leads to yelling, screaming and hitting.

Remember, first we want to see the child's "lostness," so we can regain a warm feeling and not take it personally. The child has lost her bearings; we want to keep ours. Next, we want to help relieve her suffering. Then, we want to help her see how, when she gets out of control, she is the one who suffers.

With a calm, loving tone we might say something like, "Sweetheart, you have to relax about this a little. You're getting carried away now. Look at yourself. You're making yourself so upset that you're frightening yourself. You need to calm down, sweetheart, so maybe we'll go back to your room and talk a little, or maybe you need to lie down for a bit."

Later, when calm, we can say, "Sweetheart, when things happen that you don't like, you have to learn to not get as upset as you do now. You have to understand that getting upset happens to all of us, and we all have to learn to get over it and calm down. We have to learn to not get so upset in the first place. You have to learn to deal with it so you don't get so caught up like you just were. We can help, if you want, by telling you what we do." [See Chapter IV— states of mind]

Being forced to reckon with the limit of bedtime made this discussion possible.

CONSEQUENCES?

If children won't go to bed, a natural result occurs: The kids will be tired. They may not function well. They may be crabby and irritable. Over time, they may weaken their immune systems and get sick. To avoid these, some parents learn to use logical consequences. They ask, "What will make children go to bed if they won't go on their own?"

We could ask a more productive question. Reverse it! "Why would a child not want to go to bed?"

Suppose we had resorted to some logical consequence, and later we learned that the child resisted going to bed because he felt insecure. In such a case the use of consequences would only intensify his insecurity. Had we stepped back before relying on consequences, we might have seen the child's insecurity. If we saw it, rather than apply consequences we would want to help minimize his insecurity.

Suppose, when we stepped back, we learned that our child did not want to go to bed because he didn't need to; that he was not tired yet. Should we use consequences? What if, developmentally, he is outgrowing the bedtime we had set for him, and the bedtime needs renegotiation? What if he were ready to stay up for another half hour or hour? We could say, "We're willing to try letting you go to bed later, but we'll see how you react in the morning. If you're too tired, or you're crabby, then we'll have to go back to the way it is now." Consequences would have clouded the issue.

Suppose we learned through observation that our child didn't want to go to bed because he wanted to be spending more quality time with us, suppose he needed more attention from us. Would consequences be in order? I think not. Maybe we only need to spend a little more time with him around bedtime, perhaps a half-hour lying in bed reading or talking together. Relying on consequences may have killed this wonderful opportunity.

Suppose our child didn't want to go to bed because he wanted to watch a particular TV program that comes on past his bedtime. Every night? Are consequences in order? Why would they be? That's what VCRs are for. If the parent doesn't have a VCR, or if one "important" program is in question, is there harm in letting him watch it? After stepping back and weighing what feels right, we can decide what is best. We can be flexible, so long as it does not compromise his ability to function. Consequences here would inhibit negotiation.

Suppose we observe that bedtime has become the battleground of wills; that our child uses bedtime as an act of defiance. Consequences must be in order here, right? Not necessarily! What would happen if we were to reverse the process, remove the battle? We might say—

"Okay, we've been having trouble around bedtime, and what we've been doing has not been working. From now on, you can go to bed any time you want."

"You're kidding, right?"

"No. Really."

"What's the catch?"

"Nothing."

So our ten-year-old stays up until 2:00 a.m. before dropping off to sleep on the couch from exhaustion. The next day he can barely move, but he still has to fulfill his obligations, such as going to school. At school he can barely stay awake. He comes home crabby. If he starts to take a nap, we might wake him up. "It's time to play now." That night he tries to stay up late again, but he drops off a little earlier. The next day it repeats. Chances are that within a week he will end up going to bed at a reasonable hour. No consequences were applied, but he learned an important lesson. If we had applied consequences we may have given him something else to be defiant and willful about.

Often, we are too quick to use consequences.

If we do use consequences, we have to ask ourselves whether those consequences violate rapport, respect, and trust, whether they make our kids run scared. **Anything** that adds an element of fear defeats the purpose. Anything that creates humiliation lowers kids' spirits. We want to avoid this, because we want our children to function at their best.

We can spell out guidelines and responsibilities. We can ask if they understand. We can keep our eye on it until they do it. If not, we can ask, "What happened here?" and make adjustments. Consequences may not be necessary.

A STATE OF PUZZLEMENT

All kids want to do their best. If they don't, some reason exists. Let's say a kid has a habit of rebelliousness. It would be important to deal with the issue of rebellion. Yet, we're confused about what to do. How might we get to the heart of the issue? One way is to admit that we don't understand.

We could say, "I'm puzzled about why you feel the need to talk back to me. Apparently I'm not understanding something, and I'd really like to. Tell me what I don't understand." If we get no response, we might continue with, "Is it that you _____?" She'll usually tell me if I'm wrong. "Well, what is it then? I really want to understand."

If we've talked about the need for cleaning up around the house, and the child appears to comprehend why it's important, yet he still does not clean up after himself, this is puzzling. We could say, "Kiddo, I'm puzzled by this. I talk to you about cleaning up and you don't. Is something wrong?"

Sincerely being in a state of puzzlement opens people up to new possibilities. They themselves may not know why they behave as they do until we call their behavior into question. It can move them to a higher level of understanding.

RESOLVE

Dr. Pransky also insists that we need resolve. Resolve is persistence from a healthy frame of mind—how firm we are about insisting that something happens and sticking with it. **How much resolve we have in any situation determines how cooperative and responsive our kids will be.**

We can approach kids out of weakness (anger, irritation) or out of resolve. With resolve, we clearly see what we want and hang in there until they get the message.

Some people equate anger with resolve; that our kids know how resolved we are by how much anger we show. Not true! We can be angry, then let our kids off the hook. Conversely, we can be just as resolved with calmness and clarity as we can with anger, and it works better. When angry, we act out of weakness. Out of weakness we tend to act with force, intimidation, or coercion. Our kids feel threatened and react. Instead, we want action out of strength and clear-headedness because this is what leads children to understanding.

We each have choices about how we see our children. If we see them as defiant and self-centered, we take what they do personally. The narrower our perspective the more "me-oriented" we are, and the more we act out of weakness. Instead, if we were to watch the way our children act as if we were watching a movie, we would see what they do with interest and humor. Humor feels a lot better than unpleasant feelings.

Lying on a beach with warm sun upon us, usually we are completely relaxed. The reason we are so relaxed is because we have nothing on our minds. Having nothing on our minds is our most relaxed state. To carry around concern and worry about our kids is to lose that relaxed state. If they then do something that fits our concern, we are coiled and ready to strike. We are off balance. Instead, we want to remain clearheaded and be resolved from that perspective.

CREDIBILITY

Dr. George Pransky refers what he calls the "Credibility index."

If we tell kids to do something, and they don't do it and nothing happens, the next time they will wait to see if we really mean it before they act. We will have less credibility. If we lose our credibility it can escalate to the point where they won't even hear what we say.

Taking a step back, what does it say to a child when we say something and don't mean it? What message does it give when we say we're not going to let a child do something and then we let her do it. What does it mean when we say that if she doesn't come now we're going to leave her behind, and then we don't. If we say something, we've got to mean it, or we continue to lose credibility.

It is unwise to tell children to do something that they are not going to end up doing. Therefore, we need to be careful what we ask of them. If we order it, it must be enforceable; otherwise it is best not to ask. Sometimes, inadvertently, we can ask our kids to do things that are inappropriate to their age, such as asking a three-year-old to remember to pick up his toys after a TV program is over. Sometimes we tell them things that are unrealistic, such as, "You're grounded for the next ten years." .

By the time our kids are ready to deal with some of the toughest issues, such as hanging out with the "wrong crowd," or drugs, we would be well-advised to have good credibility.

Credibility comes with sticking to what we say. Credibility comes when we get behind something and mean it, and when we follow through. If a kid doesn't do something we ask, we might first say something like, "You probably didn't remember this, but I asked you to clean the living room." This allows them to regroup while keeping our credibility high, because we're not forgetting it.

Sometimes we can require something that, in retrospect, was a mistake, such as saying a that kid cannot hang out with a certain group of friends. True, we may not like this group of friends. We may think they're a bad influence. But what we really care about are his own behaviors. To say he can't hang out with a group is often unrealistic because at school, for example, he will hang out with those friends when we're not around to see it.

If we make a mistake requiring something like this, we can admit it. "I'm sorry, I shouldn't have required that of you. It was unrealistic. But here's what troubles me about your hanging out with this group. I'm concerned that some of their behaviors, that are against the law, will rub off on you. I'm concerned that you'll be in the wrong place at the wrong time when they get busted, and it will be guilt by association. What I do care about are your own behaviors. I simply cannot accept certain behaviors. I care too much about what happens to you. Maybe we can come to a meeting of the minds about this." Here, our credibility has been restored.

Kids need to have respect for "the writing on the wall." If we say it, we've got to mean it. Otherwise, we lose credibility and it is far better not to have said it in the first place.

BREAKING THE PATTERN

Suppose we have treated our children in ways that, in retrospect, we now see were detrimental. We see how our actions have contributed to their defiance. Suppose we decide to change, to approach the child differently. Here we need patience, because the child has expectations based on what happened in the past. **He will continue to act the same way until he realizes it's a new ball game.** A change may not happen overnight. It takes commitment and persistence.

If a pattern has built over time, if we want the kid to change, we may have to change. We can go to a child and say, "I can see that I've been handling things in the wrong way and that it has caused problems. I'm really sorry. I want it to change. From now on I'd like us to talk things out so we can end up with a meeting of the minds instead of a battle. What do you think?"

Because we're starting fresh, we can forgive everything that happened in the past. This clears the decks. Now, we are drawing the line anew, and we mean it. Saying, "Is there anything that you need from me that will help you stop doing this, or can you do it on your own?" might be a real shock, but it may help to move things forward.

WHEN THINGS HAVE GOTTEN OUT OF HAND

A friend of ours, Harriet, a single mother with four children, was at her wits end. She knew that her fifteen-year-old daughter, Emily, was drinking, smoking marijuana, in all probability taking LSD, having unprotected sex with her boyfriend (who had already been picked up by police for attempting to rob a store), being disruptive in school, failing subjects, often being truant, and being generally incorrigible at home. Whenever her mother attempted to take control Emily would fight, sometimes with her fists. In short, the situation had gotten completely out of hand. Harriet expressed grave concern about the effect this must be having on her three younger children. She sought my advice.

I asked Harriet what she had done to try to intercede.

Harriet told me that she tried to set limits, but Emily scoffed at her and didn't obey. For example, when Harriet wouldn't drive Emily to see her boyfriend, Emily attempted to jump out of the car going 50 miles an hour until her mother relented.

Harriet said that she showed Emily love. She told Emily that no matter what she did she would always love her, but that her behavior was unacceptable and had to stop. Emily ignored her.

Harriet said that when she was in a low mood she tried not to talk with Emily, but sometimes she couldn't help it when things got out of control. She had said to Emily, "We've got to talk this out. Things can't go on like this." Emily sassed her back.

Harriet tried to take Emily to counseling at "youth services," but after a couple of sessions Emily refused to go back because "they won't tell me what I should do."

Since Harriet asked for assistance, let's take a step back and ask ourselves what we know.

* First, the drinking, the drugging, the sex, the truancy, the disobedience, the incorrigibility, are only the secondary problems. They are merely symptoms of the larger problem of insecurity. For some reason, Emily feels so insecure that she thinks the only way she can have fun, or for that matter get by in life, is to act in these ways. Emily is hurting badly, and her actions are only manifestations of her pain.

* Harriet may think she is showing her daughter love, but her daughter is not feeling it. Fist-fights at home are not exactly the embodiment of living in an environment of love. This relationship has no rapport. Instead of a meeting of the minds, they have a butting of the heads.

* Clearly, Emily is not connected to her innate health and common sense. She is too caught up to see it. When her mother tries to land on her, Emily scrambles to protect herself. She loses herself.

* Unless something changes with Emily's thinking, the behaviors will never change. If Emily's thinking changes the behaviors will follow.

* Even though Harriet knows that when she is in a low mood she shouldn't try to control or talk with Emily, Harriet can't help herself (or at least thinks she can't), so she does.

* Harriet is not listening deeply enough to Emily to know what the real, underlying problem is. She does not understand Emily's world, how Emily sees it, so how could Harriet possibly know the best thing to do?

* Somewhere along the line Emily did not learn respect. She does not respect her mother. Emily does not believe that her mother will follow through with her threats, so she has her over a barrel.

* Even though Harriet didn't mention this, I also knew something else. Harriet's house was in chaos, cluttered beyond recognition. It was not conducive to calm, sane living. Emily couldn't stand being there, yet she was not willing to help her mother out to make the house more sane. Emily didn't see the point or the benefit. Further, the house reflected the state of Harriet's mind.

If this is what we know, how should Harriet proceed?

First, how much is Harriet willing to change? If Harriet truly wants a change in Emily, how much is she willing to get all the points above back on track. If she isn't willing, she cannot expect much change from Emily.

Further, Harriet is so overwhelmed about her own life that she needs help herself. If nothing in her own thinking changes she will continually feel overwhelmed. She will continue to feel that everything, including Emily, is out of control. Unfortunately, to her detriment, Harriet is an expert at making things appear okay. She has been to therapists and pulled the wool over their eyes. [Note: A Psychology of Mind therapist might be able to help Harriet see the power of her own thinking to see herself and her daughter anew and perhaps some of her hidden, detrimental thinking would reveal itself, because Psychology of Mind is based on the same principles as this book.] .

Harriet told me that she was willing to get help for herself, but she never followed through. My guess is, she never intended to. Given that Harriet won't go out of her way to change, is there anything she can do for Emily?

While not ideal, Harriet could still change Emily's course by changing the way she deals with all points listed above. Nothing Harriet has tried so far has worked. She has zero credibility with Emily. Therefore, nothing that Harriet has already tried should be used again. Harriet needs to reverse the process.

If Emily is acting out of insecurity, the antidote is security. Emily needs love and acceptance for who she is, deep down inside. Harriet believes she is showing love, but she isn't showing it in the moment so that Emily feels it. Harriet needs to find that loving feeling in her heart for her daughter. She needs to see beyond the presenting behavior to that inner health, to the way Emily was as a beautiful little baby. She needs to see the lostness. When she feels it, and when it feels like the right moment, when no one else is around, she needs to have a heart-to-heart talk with Emily. But Harriet's heart must be in the right place. Is she in a good state of mind? Does she feel love in the moment? Does she see Emily's innocence and her distress? When Harriet truly sees Emily's distress, her heart will go out to her. In will rush a warm feeling. This is the time to talk.

Through an honest, respectful discussion Harriet and Emily need to come to a meeting of the minds. Harriet needs to listen very carefully to what makes Emily behave the way she does. But Emily won't tell her if asked directly. She may not know, herself. What doesn't Emily understand? Why shouldn't she talk back to her mother? Why should she do her homework? None of her friends do! Why shouldn't she have sex or take drugs? All her friends do and they don't look any worse off to her. [Third edition note: She didn't know then that some of them would end up becoming heroine addicts.] Why should she take care of herself at all? Why not just commit suicide? What does she care about? Where can a meeting of the minds be found?

Suppose no meeting of the minds can be found. Suppose Emily doesn't respond. Suppose Harriet won't even have this kind of talk. Suppose she says, "We've already had talks and they don't work." Can she still be helped with Emily?

Something can still be done, although even less ideal. When things seem to be getting out of hand, sometimes children may need to be brought up short to get their attention. Harriet needs to take charge.

She could say something like, "Emily, honey, I love you so much! I care about you so much! In fact so much that I can't bear to see you damage your life. But I've tried everything I know how. I don't know anything else to do. I'm so sorry we've gotten into fights. That's not right. That's not the way I want to be with you. This is not the way I want to live. I didn't know anything else. I hope you can forgive me."

149

At this point Harriet would want to watch Emily's reaction very carefully. If there is any possible meeting of the minds at this point, Harriet should grab it and listen very carefully, talk it out and see what conclusions they can reach together about how things can be different.

If no meeting of the minds can be found and nothing improves, Emily needs to learn that her mother is serious about a new course of action, and that she will follow through. Harriet needs to ask herself, "Okay, Emily is not obeying anything I ask. What does she want from me? Money? The use of the car? To be taken places when she wants to go?

Harriet has to be willing to take a stand. With a loving feeling Harriet can continue with something like, "Emily, honey, I decided that I am no longer willing to be treated the way you're treating me. This may not be right, but from now on, if you want something from me, you have to treat me with respect. I can no longer go on like this. All I know is that I am no longer willing to put up with you treating me like dirt and having your brothers and sisters learn this behavior from you. So if you continue as you have been, if you want to go places you can find your own transportation. If you want money, you can earn your own. You can do what you want, but don't expect me to provide you with what you want. Living together is a two-way street. I will give you food, clothing, shelter, and love, but that's all I have to do. From now on, that's all I will do. As soon as you change, I'll go back to providing what you want."

Suppose Emily still does not respond. Suppose she says she doesn't care whether her mother gives her anything or not, and her behavior remains as outrageous as ever or gets worse. Is there anything else that Harriet can do? There is, but only if Harriet is willing to resort to drastic measures. If

Harriet were only willing to change course, what follows would not be necessary.

Emily may need to be startled out of her world. Right now Emily's world is working in her favor. It protects her. She's having fun. She's getting away with what she wants. Sure, she has fights with her mother from time to time, but it doesn't get in her way too much. Emily needs to be shocked.

Still with a loving, caring feeling Harriet could say something like, "So Emily, honey, I don't know what to do here. I don't know if this is right or not, but I've decided that I cannot accept you doing these things if you're here under my care. So the next time you do something that I consider damaging to you or to this family, I have no choice but to call social services to put you in a shelter home for a while until we can reach some agreement on an acceptable way for us to live together and reach an agreement on acceptable behavior. God knows I don't want to do this in the worst way, but I simply don't know what else to do."

If Emily's behavior doesn't change, Harriet must follow through, no matter how painful it is. This cannot be an idle threat. Some people would call this, "Tough Love." Emily must understand that the door is always open. There is always another chance to work things out.

Hopefully this drastic measure will not be necessary. Hopefully, Emily would suddenly realize that the line is drawn in the sand. She will understand what will happen if she doesn't change. Because her mother is using a completely different tone and a completely different approach Emily may sit up and take notice and say to herself, "Oh wow, mom is really serious here!" This realization would give Emily an opportunity to get back on track without her mother having to implement the extreme.

If Emily tries to call her bluff, Harriet needs to get right on the phone and make that call.

Please remember that this drastic measure is only suggested when things have gotten so far out of hand that the parent truly does not see any other way. Some time in a temporary shelter may give both parties the time they need to step back enough to regain common sense and decide what they want for themselves. Later they can come together knowing what is on the line and what needs to happen. In most cases, clearer heads will prevail.

This also implies that Harriet will have had to do some homework beforehand to learn what her options are if a child is without or beyond the control of her parents.

Before taking this drastic action, if Harriet is truly concerned about having a breakthrough with her daughter and having this situation not adversely affect the life of her family, she must take a huge step back. She needs to ask herself, "What about the way this family lives and interacts with each other makes it difficult for Emily to want to be here?" The idea is not to analyze the answer but to put the question on the back burner of her mind, and go about her business. An answer will surface when she least expects it She needs to truly listen for an answer but her mind must be clear enough to hear it.

Through listening Harriet may see that Emily can't stand the chaos in that house, the mess, and she wants to escape it all. What is Harriet willing to change? What is she willing to do differently to make this home a more comforting, calm, loving, inviting place to be. Why wouldn't a child want to be in her own home?! Why would she want to be on the run all the time? There is always a reason. Emily is not the only one with the problem. It takes two to tango, two to create the difficulties.

Ultimately, at this point, Harriet has at least three choices: 1) She can keep things as they are and stay tortured by Emily; 2) She can have Emily removed from the home; 3) She can show her daughter that she is willing to put herself out to change. Of course, Harriet can only change if her thinking changes. If she takes a step back, sees what she needs to do, and finds she can't do it, she may need help. How important is this to her? Harriet can only answer that for herself.

To have privileges be dependent on responsibilities is not unreasonable, so long as the two are linked by common sense. Yet, to work best, even this must be conducted within the proper environment and after the rest of the learning process has been tried. Finally, having a child removed from the home is, obviously, a measure of absolute, last resort, to be used only when things are so out of control that no other choice appears possible. None of it would be necessary if Harriet would only go through each of the points made earlier and adjust accordingly.

DISCIPLINE WITH O.P.C. (Other People's Children)

Teachers, coaches, camp counselors, youth workers and others who work with and are in a position of authority over other people's children will find the approach offered in this book most productive as well. Disciplining other people's kids will work best if four components are in place (assuming a respectful, caring, lighthearted environment, and waiting for a clear head before disciplining):

1. **Reflect on how you are seeing the child**. Are you seeing the kid as "up to no good" or as "well-meaning and wanting to do his or her best but insecure and not knowing a better way." Get your head in the right place.

2. **Be sure the child understands his/her health**. Probably, you will have seen the child behave well in

similar situations or at different times—even if briefly. That means the child has it in him or her. You know the child is capable of behaving well and doing well, because you've seen it. And even if you haven't, you can imagine it. That health is there to come out at any time. That's who the child really is—deep down inside. The child must understand this. "Sweetie, I know you can do it because I've seen you. I know you have it in you. That's who you really are inside!"

3. **Help the child be in a state of puzzlement about his/her behavior.** In other words, if the child knows the rules and knows what is expected and has this health inside, it is very puzzling why he would violate that understanding. Something must be going on that you aren't seeing. Very likely, the child does not see it either. The idea here is to explore deeper until the child discovers something new." I know you know the rules and want to do well. Given that, is it puzzling to you that you would do that? What do you make of that? When this happens to you, do you feel it coming on beforehand or does it just sneak up on you and catch you totally by surprise? Is there any way you can catch it when it first starts to come on?" In one conversation like this, one child described that he had a "bad spot" inside him that seemed to take him over sometimes. We were then able to explore further what that meant to him

4. **If the child still insists in behaving inappropriately, have progressively increasing sanctions that are enforced.** The child must understand that she will not get away with continuing the same unacceptable behaviors over and over again. Yet, the child can be helped to see this in increments that allow her the opportunity to respond before the sanctions get worse. "Okay, you've shown no interest in behaving appropriately and don't seem to be willing to improve it, so here's what will happen if it

happens again. And the next time, here's what will happen [etc.] But I have faith in you that it won't have to get to that point, and I'm willing to help you in any way I can."

AND IN THE END . . .

This book is based on the premise that in nearly every situation that arises parents will know what to do—if they listen closely to their hearts.

To hear what is in our hearts, all we need to do is to step back, disengage, quiet the mind, clear the head—in whatever way we can. To enhance our potential for insight, we can ask ourselves the right questions to prepare our minds to receive the answers we need.

We want to know in our hearts that we and our children have an internal state of health that contains wisdom and common sense. We want to help our children tap into it. If we help them calm down, they can access it more readily. We also want to help draw out their health out by creating around them the loving, caring, supportive, respectful, lighthearted environment with which their health resonates.

We want to be aware of our feelings and moods in the moment, so we know the appropriate time to take action or speak.

We want to remember that children act out or act troubled because of insecurity, so we want to help them regain their security.

We want to listen deeply to the meaning behind our children's words, so we know how to proceed.

We want to teach them what they need to understand to get along in the world.

We want them to know with certainty what is expected, what is important to us and where we draw the line, and we want to patiently teach them and stick with it until it becomes part of them.

In so doing, we will be bring out the best in our children, and they will demonstrate it through their behavior.

The rest is merely detail.

Now, read this book again, and have a great time with your kids!

KEYS TO PARENTING FROM THE HEART

Be sure that your children are **living in an environment of love**, caring, support, respect, lightheartedness.
Understand that the feeling you have in the moment when interacting with your children is the environment that your children are living in.

See your children as always having **the health**, wisdom, and common sense deep within that is ready to be actualized at any moment.

See your children's troubling behavior as thoughts that your children are unaware of that have made them innocently get off track and lose their way. **See the lostness and innocence.**
See that your children are always doing the best they know how at the time, given the way they are seeing things.

See yourself in your moods, and understand that if you are in a low mood your thinking cannot be trusted; therefore, back off and regain perspective before taking action.
See your children in their moods and understand that when they say or do things out of an insecure, reactive state there is no need to take it personally; it is only their mood talking.

See your children's **troubling behavior as** acting out of **insecurity**; therefore help them feel more secure.
Watch your children with interest, as if watching a movie, as opposed to being caught up in their craziness.

Before you teach or discipline, do what you have to do to **clear your head and step back and observe**, so your common sense and wisdom can be available to guide you.

Help children learn how they are creating what they see with their own thinking, and, with it, how they feel and act.

Before taking action ask yourself, **"What message will my children be receiving** if I say or do this?"

Ask yourself, "What is most important to me concerning my children's behaviors? And Where do I need to draw the line?" Patiently guide your children to that end, with love.

157

APPENDIX.   IF YOU INSIST . . .*

Despite what this book suggests about the fallacy of relying on parenting techniques, some parents still insist upon using them. Despite that when parents need techniques most they are least likely to have their wits about them to apply them, and that when parents have access to their wisdom they don't need techniques, some parents still feel lost without them. Despite the implication that the answer lies in the technique outside the parent, instead of inside his or her own heart, some parents will not be satisfied that what is offered in the main body of this book is enough.

Many parents who rely on techniques appear to be in a battle. As if in a chess game, they use maneuvers and counter-maneuvers. They anticipate how the enemy will try to get them; in turn, they try to outwit the enemy and protect themselves. The problem is, the enemy is their own children.

If parents have applied conscientiously what appears in the main body of this book, this appendix is completely unnecessary and will get in the way. For those parents, I suggest not reading further. It will be far more productive to again read chapters I through IX.

This appendix, then, is *only* for those parents who, for some reason, still feel the need to take control. The only reason I offer it is, for such parents, taking control in this way is far better than relying on physical or emotional violence or punishment to take control. Again, the real answer does not lie in control. It does not lie in techniques. The real answer lies in love transmitted. The real answer lies in the heart. This appendix is only for parents who still feel helpless or stuck. For such parents, I do not put down what is in this appendix. Many valuable approaches can be found here. It is far better than feeling lost or helpless. In fact,

---

* Note: This appendix is an edited version of parts of the "Parent Skills Education" chapter of <u>Prevention: The Critical Need</u> that pertain to discipline, and what was supposed to form the basis of my "Pocket Encyclopedia of Parenting and Discipline."

these approaches have helped many a parent, myself included (before I gained this new understanding).

This appendix is intended to be a brief, clear, concise, easy-to-understand summary of ways to encourage constructive behavior toward children offered in what I consider to be the best parenting courses (outside of Health Realization). In my opinion, the best is Dr. H. Stephen Glenn's *Developing Capable People*. Thus, this chapter draws mostly from it. Ironically, Glenn does not rely on techniques either; he emphasizes what he calls "principles" of raising self-reliant children. What follows, then, is a set of "key principles" to raise healthy, capable, competent children with few behavior problems. In other words, **parents who do not follow the rest of this book will succeed best if they follow what appears in this appendix.** There is a bit of overlap.

Children Need to Gain Healthy Self-Perceptions and Skills

Research into the causes of many different problem behaviors clearly shows that to behave in healthy and constructive ways **children need seven critical perceptions and skills.** Dr. Glenn put it together in this framework, although I included some terms used by other researchers.

Healthy self-perceptions:
1. **I am a worthwhile and competent person, capable** of figuring things out for myself. I can make it without being dependent on others.
2. **I am important. I belong**. I am a significant contributing part of, or have a stake in, something greater than myself. My life has meaning and purpose.
3. **I have power to affect what happens to me.** I have control over my life.
Skills to–
4. handle ourselves from within, as in **self-discipline** and self-control;
5. interact with others, as in **communication**, cooperation, negotiation, listening;

6. deal with the world around us, as in **responsibility** and adaptability;

7. deal with abstract concepts (safe-dangerous, right-wrong, appropriate-inappropriate, good-bad, values), as in **judgment**.

Where do these self-perceptions and skills come from? Primarily from how children are treated in the family and school. If young people have not gained what they need from home or school, they will attempt to get their needs met in other ways, usually through the peer group. If we want our children to behave appropriately and be reasonably successful, our job is to help these healthy perceptions and skills emerge. What follows will help parents accomplish this.

Using the Appropriate Response at the Appropriate Age

Parents need to know that children are developmentally incapable of doing certain things at certain ages. Knowing this provides clues about how we should deal with them. Consider these brief, general rules of thumb:

Ages 0-4: These children operate by instinct. They respond to immediate stimulus-response. Little children naturally explore their worlds and get into things. If what they are doing is inappropriate, we need to show them, such as "Honey that's something you shouldn't do. If you do, here's what will happen." And, "I like it when you do that."

Ages 5-6: These children are able to delay their responses a little. They can deal with immediate implications (What will happen to me now if I do this now?). At this stage it's appropriate to give a cue and delay the negative response a bit. "If you're doing something you shouldn't, I'll count to three, and if you're still doing it, here's what will happen."

Ages 6-8: These children can begin to understand cause and effect (What could be possible outcomes for me?). "If you don't pick up your toys, you can't be in here playing."

Ages 8-12 and up: These kids are usually capable of dealing with abstract concepts, and can understand how someone else might feel. They can begin to deal with values, morals, and they can respond to reasonable consequences.

Ages 13-17: Sometimes it seems as if teenagers forget everything they've ever learned. Their bodies and minds are undergoing extreme, rapid change. They become selfish because they're trying to figure out who they are. They are preparing themselves to leave the nest but don't know how to go about it. This is natural and we shouldn't take it personally. Most eventually grow out of their craziness.

At every stage it is natural for kids to push the limits to see how far they can go. Dr. William Glasser, whose work is also drawn upon in this appendix, reminds us that if children didn't have the need to break free and move forward, we would still be in caves mindlessly doing what our parents wished. Progress has been made because children are willing to struggle to get their needs met, regardless of their parents.

This is not to suggest that we should be permissive, where nothing is clear and where a child learns to manipulate whatever he can to get around things. Nor should we be being overly strict where the kid's life is so controlled s/he never has the opportunity to learn from her own experiences. Within certain clear limits that we will enforce, kids should have the latitude to explore and learn for themselves, provided there is no danger.

We all blow it with our kids sometimes (usually it's when we're tired or irritable or when we think we don't have enough time), but we can make up for it later by apologizing and then going back and applying concepts. Jane Nelsen, author of *Positive Discipline*, says, "Mistakes are wonderful opportunities to learn." Steve Glenn says, "If we can just do one of these things one time during the course of the year, it is 100% better than not doing them at all." However, the more we apply them, the better off we'll be.

Building Capability

No matter how we discipline kids, it will work best in an atmosphere that promotes healthy self-perceptions. Certain critical "principles" of parental behavior toward children can help establish this atmosphere.

* Begin with the child's perception (then share ours)

Beginning an interaction with the child's perception instead of our own ensures that we understand the full picture before we act. We can't assume we know what our child is perceiving; we may not even be seeing the same ballpark. Next, we can share our own perception. In this way, we have a common basis for moving forward.

Beginning this way creates a nonthreatening atmosphere. If we want our children to benefit from our accumulating knowledge, our children need to be open to that learning. Our first order of business is to be sure our child is not threatened by our approach, because whenever there is perceived threat, no learning can take place.

Whenever we come upon any situation, instead of uttering an "adultism," such as "Why can't you ever do a thing I tell you?" or "How many times do I have to tell you?" or "Grow up!" if we begin with the child's perception, we minimize perceived threat and will understand better what might be contributing to his behavior.

Here is an example cited by Dr. Glenn: If I say to my 11 year old, "Please clean the living room", that sounds clear, doesn't it? There's one problem. My son may have a different perception than I do of what a "clean living room" means, or what "clean" means. My perception of "clean" might be: put the pillows back on the couch neatly, straighten up the magazines, dust the shelves, put the toys away, vacuum the floor. My child's perception of "clean" might be: push the toys to the side and sweep the floor. So that's what he does.

I come home, see the pillows and magazines still in disarray, see more dust than before I left, see the toys still in the room, and allow my perception to dictate my response: "I thought I told you to clean the living room. Don't you ever do what I tell you!? You lazy good for nothing!"

163

My kid has tried. The first time this happens he might say, "Maybe dad was just in a bad mood." The second time something similar happens, he may say, "I think there's a pattern developing here!" By the third time he may be thinking, "I'm worthless. I couldn't figure it out right. I let him down." or, "That jerk better not do that to me again." Either way, I have not set up the most conducive conditions for future behavior.

Instead, when I land in the living room, suppose I take a deep breath and say to myself, "Okay, we may have had different ideas of what a clean living room is." So I approach him. In my most caring voice, I say:

P: Honey, what was your understanding of what I meant when I said, "Clean the living room?"

C: You know, get the toys out of the way and sweep the floor.

P: Oh wow, I didn't notice that before! Now that you mention it I can see you did a good job of that, and I appreciate it. I was thinking of some other things I forgot to make clear, like straightening out the pillows and magazines, dust the shelves, and putting the toys away.

C: All that?

P: Is that too much?

C: Well..., maybe. It's a lot.

P: Okay, what about if I help you do the rest of it now. We can do it together, then next time we can talk about what we both think needs to be done beforehand, and how you'll go about doing it. Sound reasonable?"

Which of the two approaches is more likely to get my child to clean the room next time?

In summary, beginning with the child's perception is saying things like, "Honey, what was your understanding of what I wanted done here? or "Kiddo, what did we agree to here?" or "Sweetie, what do you think needs to be done now? or "What do you think happened?" A term of endearment like "honey" or whatever feels natural can be one way to reduce perceived threat. A caring tone of voice is essential.

If we approach children this way, we may be surprised how they react. At first they may be in shock at suddenly being treated in this new, respectful way. Initially they may be suspicious, but once they trust it, they'll usually respond.

* Help Young People Explore and Analyze Situations, and Make Plans

The purpose here is to help young people learn from experiences and apply what they have learned to other situations; to learn a process by which they can solve problems and plan.

The process begins with showing small children how to do things, then doing it with them for a while. As they grow older, young people need to understand the what, why, and how of an experience. One way we can help achieve this is by using the E.I.A.G. approach:

Experience – Allow kids to have experiences. So...Something happens.

Identify – Help kids identify WHAT about the experience is significant, using a question something like: "What happened?"

Analyze – Help kids understand WHY the experience happened, why it was significant, why they felt as they did as a result. The problem is, when young people are asked, "Why?", they often say "I don't know" because they feel threatened somehow. So we might have to ask this question differently, something like: "What caused that to happen?" Or, for good experiences, we could say: "What made that work out?"

Generalize – Once people understand an experience, they need to understand HOW to apply that learning to other situations: "What could you do differently next time to be sure it doesn't happen again?" "What might you need to think about next time so it will work out better?" For good experiences, a question might be, "What do you need to do next time to be sure it works out well again?"

This process should be used where possible before an experience (exploring) and after an experience (analyzing). Our tone must convey that we are truly interested in helping them figure out what's best.

165

To take this process a step further, Glasser suggests that we can convey that no matter what the difficulty we will work it out, and a plan will have to be made accordingly.

Building Power, Self-Discipline and Responsibility

* Set Reasonable Limits and Consequences (where possible) **in Advance** (and plan for what might go wrong)

The more that young people know what is expected of them and what will happen if they choose not to do what's expected, the more life becomes predictable, and the more they can see how the decisions they make affect what happens to them. If we want our children to obey rules that we believe are necessary for their safety and well-being, we must first be sure these rules are clear from the perspective of the child.Often this isn't enough. Unanticipated problems may arise. Excuses can throw a monkey wrench into the best laid plans, so it's best not to accept excuses. This means we have to do some planning beforehand. If our teenager is supposed to bring the car home with at least a quarter of a tank of gas, but it gets too late and all the gas stations are closed, could we have anticipated this possibility beforehand and planned for it so we won't be left with the problem after the fact? Maybe we could agree that if he leaves a note on the car saying he'll take care of getting gas first thing in the morning, and he does it, that would be reasonable. Whatever we end up doing, we need to be prepared for as many problems as possible by trying to predict what could go wrong: "Can you think of any other reason you might not be able to get gas into the car tonight?" – then plan for those possibilities.

Sometimes even this isn't enough. If it is not clearly understood in advance what the consequence will be if he chooses not to respect the limit, we have nothing to fall back on. If we're concerned about our sixteen-year-old's safety if she's about to go out on a date late at night, we might set a curfew. "Honey, we need you to understand that the privilege of going out depends on your responsibility to be home at a reasonable time, so we don't have to stay up worrying about you. What time

166

do you think is reasonable?" If she says 3:00 a.m. we might say, "Well that's not reasonable to me. I was thinking of 10:00 p.m. [or whenever, then I may be willing to negotiate]. So I expect you home at 11:00 p.m. Is that understood?"

Okay so far, but remember, we've got to plan for contingencies. "Now, if something unpredictable should happen where it doesn't look like you'll be able to make it home on time, we expect a call from you before 11:00 p.m. to tell us what the problem is, okay?"

That sounds okay, but suppose our young adult, for whatever reason, does not come home on time and does not call? The kid walks in. We confront her. She has some excuse. What do we do then?

We are trying to develop the perception that she has the power to affect what happens to her. If she doesn't know in advance what will happen if she decides not to follow the rule, and we decide to punish her for disobeying, all power lies with us; it has been taken away from her. We've made all the decisions. Suddenly her parents are laying some punishment on her, and it becomes easy for her to blame them for what happened. She will believe that what happened to her had little to do with what she did.

On the other hand, we could continue our conversation in advance by saying, "Now, if you choose not come home by 11:00 p.m., what do you think a reasonable consequence should be?" and we discuss it and try to reach a mutual conclusion. Even if we can't agree, parents still need to ultimately draw the line. So we might say, "If you make the decision to come home after 11:00 and not call, then you will also be making the decision to stay in for the rest of the week. Is that clear?" Now the bases are covered.

Glasser would say it may not be desirable for the consequence to be for a set period of time; rather, the consequence should be applied until the child is willing to work out a plan that will ensure we won't have a problem. Younger kids may have to be removed from everyone *until* their behavior is reasonable. It might take five minutes and it might take five months, but however long it takes, it is until the kid decides he's willing to behave reasonably. For older kids, it might be loss of freedom or privileges *until* they're willing to comply. "If you ever want to go out again, we'll have to get together to work something out." Both approaches can work. It may be worthwhile to try Glasser's approach first, but if the kid tries to manipulate by continually making plans and breaking them, then a consequence for a set period of time may be in order.

* Follow Through with Respect and Caring, Being Sure the Child Understands How S/he Made the Decision

If limits and consequences have been set in advance, the only thing left to do is respect those limits, and follow through with whatever was agreed.

Once a violation has occurred there is no longer room for negotiation. If we back down at this point, they will not understand that their actions caused the consequence to occur. They will learn that it is possible to get around things and will not respect our agreements.

How we apply consequences makes all the difference. If we get angry and yell and scream, the kid will get upset with us and shift the blame. Both the limit and consequence have been set and understood in advance. What is there to be angry about? The kid made his decision. So we're free to communicate this message in the most respectful and caring way we can.

The key is to be sure our youngster understands how it was his decision to have the consequence happen. By making the decision to not come home on time and not call, he also made the decision not to go out for the rest of the week. The decision was all his. Everything was predictable in advance. He decided what would happen. The less we say, the better. Lecturing detracts from the simple point at hand.

Dr. Glenn gives the example of a teenager coming home late from an agreed to curfew:

P: Honey, what time did you understand you were supposed to be home?

T: I forget.

168

P: Well, let me refresh your memory then. We agreed you'd be home at 11:00 and that if anything happened to make that impossible, you'd call us before 11:00 and let us know. Do you remember that?"

T: I guess.

P: What was your understanding of what would happen if you didn't come home on time?

T: [Grunt] [Note: If they perennially forget, we could put it in writing and sign it.]

P: Well, we agreed that you wouldn't be going out for the rest of the week; that by making the decision to come home late, you would also be making the decision not to go out for the rest of the week. I just wanted to be sure we had the same understanding of why you wouldn't be going out this week.

That's respectful, and it's firm. We cannot back down! If he forgot that later in the week he had an important date, and now the weekend is here and he wants to go out . . .

T: I'm sorry! I'll never do it again. This is really important to me. Please!!

P: I'm sorry you didn't think of that when you made the decision to come home late. This must be upsetting to you. But I have to respect your decision.

If he goes off the wall ranting and raving about how you're hurting him, wait until he's finished, then stick to respecting his decision. What can the youngster say then? "Don't respect my decisions"? Next time if he wants the privilege of going out, he'll probably get home on time. Later, when things have calmed down, it might be good to go through the E.I.A.G with him to figure out how he might be able to avoid this difficulty next time.

Glasser does not believe in setting specific consequences in advance, only limits. Using Glasser's approach, if the teen wants to go out again, he can't until he makes detailed plans with us of what he will need to do to respect the limit next time. The predictable consequence is, if a limit is not respected, some privilege or freedom will always be lost until something reasonable is worked out. If the kid chooses not to work it out,

169

he can decide to sit at home for the rest of his life if he wants. Most kids eventually see the advantage to working things out.

* Structure Opportunities (and allow for opportunities to occur) Where Children Can Experience Either the Natural Rewards or Consequences of their Decisions

This principle complements the previous two. Children need to experience the realities of the world without being rescued from minor pains or heartaches that they would naturally encounter along the way. They need to "feel the pinch" in small ways so they'll want avoid similar, more difficult experiences next time. Children also need to feel the natural rewards and joys of good experiences.

Certain things are naturally predictable. For example, if I don't buy or grow or find food, I don't eat. No one has to tell me why I'm hungry. If I forget to put gas in my car, I run out of gas. I've had to accumulate this wisdom the hard way. After running out of gas several times I finally decided, rather than go through the pain again, that it would be wiser to put gas in the car when the tank gets low. Such "natural" consequences often work best.

Self-discipline often emerges from learning the hard way. We don't want to rob our children of this opportunity. If supper is ready and we want our young child to eat, we call her to come in. If she doesn't, rather than yelling and screaming at her to come in while keeping her dinner warm, it is best to simply go about eating and clean up. When she comes in and says, "I'm ready to eat now," or "I'm hungry," we can say kindly, "Sweetie, when it was time to eat, you felt like playing; now that you feel like eating it's time to play, so go play and try again in the morning." Many parents find this difficult to do, but we have to ask ourselves under which circumstances will children learn self-discipline? What will be their perception if they get bailed out? The kid won't starve by missing one meal, but she may feel it enough to do something differently next time.

This process can start when a child is a few days old. After a little baby has been fed, cleaned, thoroughly loved, and played with for a good amount of time, it is time for the baby to entertain herself for a while. A baby or toddler may continue to want attention, even after adequate attention has been given. We might let this baby cry on her own for a while. Once she gets the picture that the parent isn't going to bail her out at every whimper, she'll eventually stop crying and learn to entertain herself for short periods, so long as she's secure enough to know that the parent will be back soon with all kinds of attention and love. Early on she needs to learn that at times people need to be on their own and take care of themselves. It will make it easier when they get older. [Note: This does not mean neglecting the child or staying away for long periods. Even when the parent is not with the child physically, the parent still must be closely attuned to what is going on with the child. Parents must be sensitive to that different type of cry that says, something's really wrong here, and respond immediately!]

Sometimes consequences occur because of what other people impose. If we don't pay our rent, people come and evict us. If we don't pay our telephone bill, our phone gets shut off. These consequences are predictable and logical. They happen because of our actions. Conversely, when we pay our bills our lives proceed without that interruption. If we get enough sleep, we usually feel better the next day. If we act nice to others and send them loving thoughts, they generally treat us nice in return. These are little rewards that come from our actions. When we're experiencing the type of rewards and consequences that arise from the natural order we can most often accept whatever comes our way (except, perhaps if we're poor and the natural order is keeping us that way no matter how hard we work). However, if besides evicting me my landlord comes and punches me in the face, that is no longer logical or reasonable, and I'm no longer accepting. If I get caught speeding and besides getting a ticket have to write "I will not speed" one hundred times, it makes no sense. When someone interferes with allowing the logical course to unfold, we get resentful. Kids do too!

Back to the meal story, when a kid gets older and misses a meal, he is capable of making his own meal, so what would be felt naturally won't have the same impact. In such cases, we may have to impose conditions to have more of an impact. If our kid wants to cook for himself, fine, but he has to clean up after himself, and he has to eat something reasonably nutritious if he wants the privilege of using the kitchen.

Here are some subtleties in using natural and logical consequences properly:

- **Use natural consequences unless the natural consequence is too dangerous or too meaningless from the point of view of the child.**

Natural consequences often work best, but sometimes we can't afford to let the natural consequence occur. If our kid is playing in the street, we can't afford to let her experience the natural consequence of getting hit by a car, even though she would learn better that way (if she survived). Yet, if the natural consequence for keeping the living room messy is to have a messy living room and perhaps be unable to find things easily, most children are perfectly content with that state. If it holds no meaning for the child, he will probably not learn from it. In these types of situations, logical consequences might be used.

The first order of business is always to get the child out of danger. After the kid is safely out of the street, we can concern ourselves with setting up a condition where the child does not go out to the street in the first place. "If you're going to continue to play in the street, then you can't go outside at all. It's up to you." Or, "Anything left in the living room will be scooped up and taken to the Salvation Army in the morning". This is often likely to produce results, provided it is followed through.

- **The consequence must be logical and reasonable from the point of view of the child**

This is the trickiest part of applying consequences. The consequence must be related to the event. We can try to put ourselves in the child's shoes to check out whether a consequence is logical and reasonable the way our kid sees it. If a child continues to leave the door open when she goes outside, not letting her watch TV is unrelated and therefore not useful. Not being able to use the door would be logically related. She can't use the door if she continues to leave it open. [Of course if the kid then tries to use the windows, we'd have to set a rule

172

about that one.] Unreasonable consequences like not being able to go out again for the next month will breed resentment.

- If the limit and consequences have not been set in advance, use it as an opportunity to plan and set it up for next time.

When a problem arises for which a consequence has not been set in advance, we have three choices: 1. We can punish on the spot, taking from the child all power. 2. We can use the opportunity to plan together what might be a reasonable consequence, given the situation. 3. We can use the situation as an opportunity to set up the consequence the next time a similar situation arises, where there will be no confusion about what will happen. We could say, "Okay, we hadn't anticipated this, but let's be clear that the next time this happens, [such and such] will be the consequence. Is that understood?" Glasser's approach might help here as a cross between numbers 2 and 3 above: "Until we work out how to avoid this situation again, you can't go anywhere."

* Remove Children from Situations Where They Can't Control Themselves to Take Time Out or Cool Off

Sometimes children get so emotionally involved, they lose control. To help them regain control, they sometimes need to take time out to cool off for a while until they're able to settle down and behave reasonably again. For small children, this is especially useful, as an alternative to spanking.

As usual, we must take care how we put it into effect. What will be the difference if we yank them bodily from whatever they're doing and slam them into a corner, or if we pick them up gently but firmly and say, "Honey, you need to rest here for a while until you can treat others nicely again." They can be in their room, or on a chair set apart from where the action is, or wherever we think its appropriate. We are restricting their freedom of movement until they're willing to behave well. Glasser maintains that being sent to one's room shouldn't be a sentence. If there's a TV in their room, they shouldn't be deprived of that too. They need only to be away from others until they choose to follow the rules.

* Choices

This principle is inherent in the others but deserves special mention. Small children especially can relate to the concept of choices. "If you want to be with me when I'm talking on the phone then you have to be quiet so I can hear, or you can make noise in your own room. It's up to you." Little kids can be picked up and physically moved if they keep disturbing us and won't move on their own. If a defiant kid won't stay in his room, he can be held or restrained firmly but not painfully. His choice is, we'll let go when he stays where he's told, and he can join us when he decides to behave reasonably.

Bigger kids usually can't be picked up and moved, nor would we want to try. Interestingly, for large, defiant teenagers, the concept of choice works in a similar way; its just more subtle. If we've followed all the principles well, and our adolescent is still being defiant and carrying on, we have choices. Rather than trying to control the situation with brute, physical force, we could ask ourselves, "What does this young person want from me?" Does he want freedom of movement? Does he want use of the car? Does he want money from us? This is where he has a choice to make. If he wants things from us, he's got to treat us with respect. If not, we're not willing to go out of our way for him. "You can't go out until you learn to treat people in the home with respect, because we don't trust that you're able to treat people in society with respect if you can't do it here." The word "until" makes it his choice.

* For Young Children especially, Ignore the Bad Behavior As Much As Possible, And Attend to the Good Behavior

Minor problem behaviors crop up often. Sometimes, if they're not serious, its best to leave them alone and give the problems the opportunity to go away by themselves. If we jump in too quickly, we could end up escalating a problem that would have easily gone away by itself. For example when two siblings are fighting and someone is in danger of getting hurt, then it becomes a different story. We need to recognize that sometimes kids do things–even bad things–just to get our attention. We usually respond by giving them attention, by snapping at them. So they learn that's how to get attention from us.

This is particularly true in the case of whining. The purpose of whining is to get attention. Since we usually give attention by saying, "Stop whining!" we've got to reverse the process. When the whine starts, we should turn away from the whine and not say a word. However, we want to close attention to when the whine stops, then we give attention. The first time, and only the first time, we can say something like, "Thanks for stopping that whining, now we can talk." Then when the whine starts up again, we turn away. When the whine stops we respond. We keep doing this until the kid gets the picture. If we're pretty consistent about this, the whining usually stops in about a week. Later, if it starts up again, we go through the same process.

Two cautions: 1) Some kids get the idea that if they first whine and then stop, they'll get attention. The best idea is to give attention often, when the kid has done nothing special to deserve it. Remember, if we' want to give attention to the good, what's most good is the child herself, so we want to pay attention to her when not connected to any behavior. 2) If we suddenly stop giving attention for what we've always given attention to before, the kid will crank up the whine to ten times the level before it will eventually subside. We need to prepare ourselves to ride it out because it can get unbearable for a while. We can wear ear plugs if we have to. It's not easy, but not caving in pays off.

* Help Children Prepare for the Specific Decisions They Will Likely Confront In Growing Into Adulthood by Helping Them Build Resistance Through "Social Inoculation"

An inoculation means getting a small dose of a disease under controlled conditions, causing immunities to build so when the real disease comes along we will be resistant. "Social inoculation" is the same concept applied to social problems. If we prepare young people for how to deal with the problems of drugs and sex, for example, before actually encountering them, they will be better prepared to resist those problems when actually confronted with them.

Whether we like it or not, adolescents (pre-adolescents in some neighborhoods) are often forced to make decisions that can affect their minds and bodies. Kids need to be prepared for the moment they're handed their first joint, or first can of beer, or hit of crack, or get sexually propositioned for the first time, at whatever age it might be.

The social inoculation process works best if it begins when the child is very young. Different steps are taken at different stages of development, corresponding to what they are developmentally ready for, leading to the period between ages 8-12. (In the teenage years such rapid growth occurs, and teens are too immersed and emotionally involved in these issues.) The 8-12 period is critically important as a non-threatening time to learn about these issues and begin to practice how to respond to them.

Consider the example of preparing a child to resist the temptation to drink. We can begin our process very early, as soon as the child is exposed to drinking. Even 4-5 year olds get exposed to drinking on TV all the time, the implication being that drinking is good; it's the thing to do. At this stage what we want to do is simply introduce an alternative message. If problem drinking has occurred somewhere in our family (not just our immediate family), we need to be ready for a moment we see our children watching someone drink on TV and say, "Honey, I just want you to know that drinking alcohol is something people in our family haven't been able to handle very well." If there is no alcoholism in our family, we could say, "When you see people drinking on TV I just want you to know that a lot of people get into trouble when they drink alcohol", or, "That's something we don't do in this family", and walk out of the room. All we're trying to do at this point is introduce an alternative message to the "do drink" messages they're bombarded by.

When kids are between ages 5-7 and can defer gratification a little, we might say, "When you see people drinking on TV, come and get me so we can talk about it." or, "Lets remember to talk about this." At that point we can sit down and talk with them, look at drinking behavior, find out what their perception is of it, then share that when people drink sometimes it causes huge problems for themselves and their families, "So when you see that, you need to think, 'This is not something that my family can get involved with.'" If problem drinking already occurs in the home, it is more difficult. If only one parent is involved, we could say, "That's why daddy [or mommy] acts like ____ sometimes." This is not so easy when it hits so close to home, but it still needs to happen, or our child is going to learn the behavior modeled to them.

When children reach ages 8-9, this is an extremely important time for serious discussion, before they are emotionally invested. Between 8-12 is the period when kids are ready to mature in judgment and when adult influence is still high. After 12, adult influence often diminishes rapidly and peer influence increases, just when a kid becomes most at risk.

Here it is important to discuss that the 12-18 year old period is unique in a person's growth and development. Much of what our bodies grow into will be determined during this period. Once this process starts, all the hormones need to be in very delicate balance. Not only do we need rest and to eat well so we have enough resources and energy to grow well, but we also need to stay away from chemicals during this time because when chemicals mix with this process it can upset the delicate balance we need. The part of our brain most affected by drugs is the same part that handles stress, and it takes twenty or so years to stabilize so it can handle all the tensions and stresses. When alcohol or other drugs are introduced into an immature system, it's like an unstable chair: it can be knocked over more easily than a balanced chair (a mature system). From the time we're conceived we are programmed genetically to be a certain way, to grow into a certain kind of adult. If we start mixing chemicals in with that process and mess everything up, we may never get the chance to find out what our potential would have been. Our goal at this stage is to help children make a commitment to themselves that they don't want to put themselves in jeopardy by

177

possibly damaging themselves, and therefore they have no intention of drinking or using drugs during these years.

We are then ready for the final and most complicated step in the social inoculation process. We can say something like. "Honey, I know you say you're committed to not drinking, and I believe you, but lots of kids say that but then get a lot of pressure from their peers and end up doing it anyway. I can see a time in a couple of years when you're hanging out at [the favorite local hang out] and you're with your best friends, and they pull out a can of beer and offer you a drink, what will you do? Wait! Don't tell me, show me. I'll pretend I'm [his best friend] and I'll try to get you to take a drink." At this point the child might say, "Charlie wouldn't do that", and we could say, "Maybe not, but lets say he does." Then we start putting the pressure on with every conceivable argument a friend could find to get the kid to take a drink, including "You're chicken. You're a wuss!", and, "If you don't do this, I'm not gonna be your friend anymore!" These can hurt. If our kid gets stuck, we stop and have a discussion. We want to find out what he's feeling, help him figure out all the alternatives and what he can do. We can give him the benefit of our experience, and help him with refusal skills such as, "Let's [do something else], instead."

Through this process we have better prepared him for the moment it will almost inevitably happen. Otherwise he will be totally caught off guard and will often do the most expedient thing he can to survive a difficult moment.

Research shows that the longer one can delay the onset of first use, the less likely the young person will be to develop a dependency, and if they do they'll be able to kick it easier than the person who starts younger.

If this process does not seem to be working, perhaps our kid has already become involved by the time we go through this process. Once a disease comes along it's too late for an inoculation. He may need intervention. Or if a kid is heavily involved in alcohol or other drug use, we have to try to get him into treatment. Get help!

* * *

Now that you've read this appendix, forget about it and reread chapters I through IX. Don't get caught in the trap of trying to remember the technique or "to do it right." Get back to your own heart. It will be far more productive and satisfying.

AFTERWORD

Shortly before this book went to press we received this e-mail from Jaime, toward the end of her freshman year at college:

"I just want you and mom to know that you mean the world to me. I miss you very much, but I appreciate all you let me do and what you have taught me. Many people tell me how envious they are of my relationship with you, and I take it less for granted now than ever. I love you both more than words can tell. I miss you very much. Tell Dave I love him."

Bibliography

Glenn, H.S. (1988). *Raising Self-Reliant Children In a Self-Indulgent World.* Rocklin, CA: Prima Publishing.

Pransky, G. (1990). *The Commonsense Parenting Series* (audiotape series). LaConner, WA: Pransky & Associates. (360) 466-5200.

Pransky, J, (1991). *Prevention: The Critical Need.* Springfield, MO: Burrell. Available from NEHRI Publications. (802) 563-2730.

Stewart, D. and Stewart, C. (undated). Can Love Survive Commitment? (audio tape). Unavailable.

Other Recommended Readings

Banks, S. (1998). *The Missing Link.* Renton, WA: Lone Pine Publishing.

Mills, R.C. (1995). Health Realization Parent Manual. Alhambra, CA: California School of Professional Psychology Community Health Realization Institute.

Pransky, G. (1992). *The Relationship Handbook.* Blue Ridge Summit, PA: Tab Books Available from Pransky & Associates (360) 466-5200.

Pransky, J. (1998). *Modello: A story of hope for the inner-city and beyond.* Cabot, VT: NEHRI Publications.

Pransky, J. & Carpenos, L. (2000). *Healthy Thinking/Feeling/ Doing from the Inside-Out: A middle school cirriculum and guide for the prevention of violence, abuse & other problem behaviors.* Brandon, VT: Safer Society Press.

ABOUT THE AUTHOR

Jack Pransky, Ph.D. is Director of the *Northeast Health Realization Institute* and is an international consultant and trainer for the prevention of problem behaviors and the promotion of well-being. He also authored the books, **Prevention: The Critical Need** (1991), **Modello: A Story of Hope for the Inner-City and Beyond,** (1998), and co-authored the **Healthy Thinking, Feeling, and Doing–from the Inside-Out** (2000) curriculum and guide for middle school students. Pransky has worked in the field of prevention since 1968 in a wide variety of capacities. He has offered parenting training and consultation to a great number of parents, and has trained many parenting course instructors.